FINAL VERDICT

SALLY RIGBY

TOP
DRAWER
PRESS

Edited by Emma Mitchell of @ Creating Perfection.

Cover Design by Stuart Bache of Books Covered

GET ANOTHER BOOK FOR FREE!

To instantly receive the free novella, **The Night Shift**, featuring Whitney when she was a Detective Sergeant, ten years ago, sign up for Sally Rigby's free author newsletter at www.sallyrigby.com

'What's wrong with my mum? Has anything happened?' she demanded, unable to wait any longer.

'Lorraine will explain everything to you,' Riki replied in a soft voice.

She didn't pursue it. She'd been a copper long enough to know when she'd hit a brick wall. She headed over to the manager's office, knocked on the door, and waited to be called in.

The older woman behind the desk looked up and smiled. Unlike the care assistants who wore navy uniforms, she was wearing her own clothes. 'Hello, Whitney. Please take a seat.' She gestured to one of the two chairs in front of her desk.

Whitney grabbed the back of one of them, pulled it out, and sat down. 'Tell me, what is it? Why did you call me in?' She twisted around her finger the gold signet ring she wore.

'I don't want to alarm you, because we don't know anything yet, but we called the doctor in to have a look at your mother. A few days ago, a small lump was found in her breast.'

Whitney swallowed hard. 'Lump? Is it…?' She couldn't bring herself to say the word.

'It's probably nothing, but we need to make sure. The doctor has referred her to the breast care clinic for some tests.'

'Why didn't you tell me sooner? You said you found the lump days ago.' Her body tensed as she tried to process the news.

'We wanted to speak to the doctor first, before worrying you. It's standard practice.'

Not any more. She couldn't have them keeping things from her.

'From now on, I want to be kept fully informed of

2

everything, as it happens. When will she be going for the tests?' The calmness in her voice belied the panic coursing through her.

'We're not sure. Appointments can take up to two weeks to come through, depending on how busy they are.'

Two weeks? It seemed like an eternity.

'But that's ages. Is there anything we can do to put her to the top of the list?'

A rhetorical question. There was nothing to be done. If only she could have afforded private health care for her mum they might have avoided the wait.

'Hopefully it won't be too long. The doctor has sent the referral and we have to wait. Try not to worry, your mum will be seen as soon as possible.'

Whitney slumped in the chair. After everything else that had happened with her mum, she didn't deserve this. 'Does she know?'

'She knows about the lump and that the doctor has suggested she has more tests. We haven't discussed possible outcomes with her. Not at this stage.'

'How did she take it?'

'In her stride. She didn't seem unduly alarmed. We don't want you to worry her when you speak.'

'I won't. Please keep me informed. I want to know as soon as the appointment comes through because I'm going to go with her.'

'That's not necessary, if you're busy.'

'I'll be going, whatever's happening at work,' she said, a *this is not up for discussion* tone to her voice, which she immediately regretted as she knew all the staff had her mum's best interests at heart.

'We'll send a carer to go with you both,' Lorraine said in a gentle voice.

One Whitney recognised as she often used it with families of victims.

'Thank you, but it's not necessary as I'll be there.'

Whitney was grateful for everything Lorraine and her team did, but she was going to be with her mum every step of the way.

'We can discuss it once the appointment has come through,' Lorraine said.

'I'm going to see her now.' Whitney stood and left the room, not wanting to talk further, in case she burst into tears.

She headed to the day room, where her mum usually spent the morning, and drew in a deep breath, forcing her tense body to relax. It would only make things worse if her mum noticed how uptight she was. Especially if she was having one of her good days and was able to see straight through her.

The large room was pleasant, light, and airy, despite the furniture being worn, and her mum was sitting in one of the easy chairs watching the television. Morning TV had never been her thing when she was fit and healthy. But at least now it kept her occupied. She walked over to her.

'Hello, Mum,' she said. There was no answer, and Whitney swallowed.

At only sixty-five, her mum was young to be in a care home, but she'd been unable to look after herself or Whitney's brother, Rob, who was now living in a different care home. He'd been attacked in his teens and suffered irreparable brain damage. Their mum had looked after him for years, but since her own diagnosis, there was no other option but for them to move into specialist facilities. Whitney hated her family being apart, but what else could she do?

It didn't help that Whitney's daughter, Tiffany, was

overseas in Australia. Should she tell her what was happening with her granny? Or was it too soon?

'Mum?' she repeated.

Her mum finally turned, eyes glazed, and mouth set in a concerned line. Whitney's heart sank. It was clearly one of her *not so good* days.

'Hello. What are you doing here?' her mum asked, turning back towards the television.

'I've come to see you.'

'I can't talk at the moment. Ellen's show is on. Can you come back later?'

Tears formed in Whitney's eyes and she blinked them away.

'It's up to you, Mum. I'm happy to stay and watch some television with you.' Whitney glanced at her watch. She'd managed to slip away as it was fairly quiet at work and she wouldn't be missed for an hour or so. She could stay if her mum wanted her there, though it didn't appear so.

Her phone rang and, grateful for the distraction, she looked at the screen. It was Claire, one of the local pathologists. What could she want?

'Give me a moment, Mum. I've got to take this phone call.'

Her mum didn't reply, just continued staring at the TV screen.

She walked away and stood by the window. Outside the garden borders were full to bursting with yellow daffodils and red tulips. She loved spring with all of its vibrant colours. It cheered everything up. Well, almost everything.

'Hello, Claire. This isn't a good time. Can I call you back?'

'No. I need to speak to you now.'

Whitney sighed at Claire's officious tone. One thing about the pathologist was she'd never cut you any slack.

'I'm with my mum at the care home,' she explained.

'How soon can you get here?' Claire asked, her voice a little softer. Maybe she did understand.

'Is it important?'

'I wouldn't be asking if it wasn't.' Forget that previous thought. The impatience in Claire's voice was evident.

'Give me thirty minutes. I'll be with you at eleven, if that's okay?' Whitney said.

She didn't want to leave her mum straight away. Surely the pathologist would understand that.

'It will have to be,' Claire said before ending the call without even saying goodbye.

That was all she needed, Claire going off on a rant. She didn't even say why she wanted to see her. There hadn't had any deaths recently involving Whitney and her team. It was probably just Claire being *Claire*.

She'd find out soon enough.

She hurried back to her mum, who hadn't moved and was still staring at the screen.

'I'm back, Mum,' she said.

'Hello, Whitney.' Her mum smiled; the foggy gaze gone. It was amazing how she could change from being *not with it* one minute to *fully alert* the next. 'What are you doing here on a Monday morning?'

It was like she hadn't remembered they'd spoken only a few moments ago.

Whitney smiled. It was good that she knew the day of the week. 'I called in to see you after visiting Lorraine. She told me they've arranged an appointment for you to see a specialist.'

'Yes, that's right. They found a lump in my breast. I'm sure it's nothing. I feel perfectly fine,' her mum said as casually as if they were discussing what to have for lunch.

'I'm coming with you when you go for the tests.' She took hold of her mum's hand and squeezed it.

'Why would you want to do that? I'm sure it will be nothing.' Her mum pulled her hand away and waved it dismissively.

It was typical of her mum to minimise it, not wanting Whitney to worry. It was what she always did. Even when money had been tight after Whitney's dad had died, her mum had played it down.

'I want to be with you, Mum. End of discussion.'

'Okay, if you can get away from work.' Her mum shrugged. 'I take it there are no murders going on at the moment.'

'Why do you say that?'

'Because that's all your work seems to be. Murders, murders, murders. But, obviously, if you're here on a Monday morning, things must be quiet.'

Whitney smiled to herself. It did seem like the only cases they had were murders. It wasn't totally true, although murders did seem to take up more of her time than most of their other work.

'You're right. It is quiet, and that's how I like it. Quite frankly, we've had enough murders over the last eighteen months to last us a lifetime.'

'You'd soon get fed up if it remained quiet. It sounds like you could do with a holiday. When did you last have some time off?' Her mum rested her hand on Whitney's arm.

'You know me. I don't do holidays. I prefer to be at work.'

Actually, when did she last have time off? Months and months ago, when she travelled with the Rock Choir to

London for a concert. Maybe she should take a break and go somewhere relaxing.

'How's Tiffany getting on? Have you heard from her recently?'

'Yes, I have. She phones me every week using WhatsApp.'

'What?' her mum said, frowning.

'It's an app you have on your phone so you can speak to people all over the world and it doesn't cost anything.'

'The things you can do these days are incredible. Technology has passed me by.' Her mum shook her head.

'Not all technology,' Whitney said. 'You can use a TV remote. You can use a phone.'

'You know what I mean,' her mum said, smiling. 'Can I speak to Tiffany? I want to find out how she's getting on.'

'Yes. I'll arrange a time for her to contact me when I'm here with you and then you can both talk. She's getting on fine and is working in a bar on the Sunshine Coast.'

'I bet the weather's nice there. Not like here. It's been so cold recently. You'd never believe we were in spring.'

'She's loving it. She's sent me photos of her and Phoebe, the friend she's travelling with.' She pulled her phone out of her pocket. 'Look.' She showed her mum some photos.

'Well, good luck to them. I wish I'd had those sorts of opportunities when I was younger, but I didn't.' Her mum let out a sigh.

Whitney glanced at her watch. 'I'd better go now. I've an appointment with the pathologist. She wants to speak to me urgently. Sorry, I can't stay longer.'

'Is it another murder?' her mum asked, her eyes bright.

Whitney smiled at her mum's response. She'd always been interested in murder cases.

'I hope not. I'll see you soon.'

'Okay, love.'

She leaned in and gave her mum a kiss.

Please let the lump be nothing.

She left the day room and walked to the front door.

'Whitney, I'm glad you're still here.' Lorraine appeared from her office. 'There's been a cancellation and your mum can be fitted in for some tests on Wednesday.'

'Wednesday? That's quick.'

It couldn't be good if they were fitting her in so soon.

'The appointment's at eleven-thirty.'

'I'll be here at ten-thirty,' she said, trying to hide her cracking voice with a cough.

She walked away from Lorraine, fighting back the tears all the way to her car. After everything that had happened with the dementia, it was ridiculous that her mum might now have cancer. It wasn't fair. After Whitney's dad had died, her mum had worked hard to look after herself and Rob and to provide for them both. It hadn't been easy, but she'd never complained. She just got on with it. Whitney had helped where she could, but she had Tiffany to take care of.

All Whitney could hope for was that it wasn't what she feared and, if it was, it had been caught early enough to treat.

Two days to wait.

Two days of non-stop worry.

Chapter Two

Whitney left the care home and went back to her car, an old Ford that had seen better days, but was all she could afford. It got her from A to B, which was all she could say about it.

She tried to put her mum's situation to the back of her mind as she drove to the morgue. What did Claire want? She'd been vague and a little strange when they'd spoken. The pathologist wasn't usually one to engage in that sort of behaviour.

There was hardly any traffic and it didn't take long to get to the hospital. Once she'd arrived, she parked and walked through the double doors leading to the morgue. The familiar antiseptic smell, that was so much a part of the place, engulfed her. Bile rose in her throat, but she choked it down. After all these years she should have been used to it, but the initial smell still made her gag.

She continued down the corridor until reaching the doors into the morgue. Claire was seated at her desk, peering at a computer screen. Her face was only inches away from it, even though she had on her glasses. As usual, the pathologist was wearing something weird and wonderful. Today it was a skirt in electric blue with cerise tights, and a white and red long-sleeved shirt. Whitney smiled to herself, the familiarity steadying her anxiety about her mum.

'Morning,' she said.

Claire visibly jumped. 'What are you doing here?' she said, turning around, her green eyes flashing with annoyance. 'I wasn't expecting you for another ten minutes.'

Whitney glanced at her watch. Claire was right. If she'd have realised she was early, she'd have stopped at the drive-through for a coffee. She certainly could do with a caffeine fix. She hadn't had one since breakfast and a lot had happened since then.

'I got here sooner than I thought. Can we talk now?'

Claire was the one who'd called her in, and yet it seemed like it was the other way around. She knew the pathologist well and understood her behaviour. They went back years and although not close friends, they had a respect for each other which went beyond their respective jobs.

'I suppose this can wait.' Claire closed the document she was working on and stood. The rather round pathologist was one of very few people at work shorter than Whitney. It was only an inch. But an inch was an inch in Whitney's book.

'Is it important?' Whitney enquired.

'It's none of your business,' Claire said.

'Only asking. What's the problem? Why did you call me in so urgently?'

'Come with me.' Claire took a white coat from the peg on the wall and slipped it on over her clothes.

They headed into the main lab area where there were

three stainless steel tables in the middle. On one of them was a body covered by a sheet.

'Over here,' Claire said. She pulled back the sheet covering a man who looked to be in his fifties. He had short dark hair, flecked with a large amount of grey.

Claire grabbed hold of the overhead light, pulled it across and turned it on, so his face and upper torso were lit. Apart from the y-shaped stitched incision from the post-mortem, Whitney could see nothing wrong with him. No bruising. No cuts. No discolouration on his face. Nothing. He appeared perfectly normal. If anything, he looked in good shape, with not an ounce of fat on him. He was also tanned, which he certainly didn't get from the British weather in spring. Had he been on holiday somewhere?

'What am I meant to be looking at?' Whitney asked, peering at the body and frowning.

'I was doing a routine post-mortem on this man because he'd died suddenly of what transpired to be a heart attack, despite him being very fit. There was no apparent damage to his arteries and internal organs. Hence the puzzle. Why did his heart give up?' Claire said, a mysterious tone to her voice.

Whitney really didn't need this subterfuge. Not today. Was Claire playing games with her?

'Why do I need to know this?' She tried to hide her frustration, but judging by the tone of her voice didn't manage to.

'Let me finish.'

'Okay. Okay. I'll humour you,' she said as she held up her hands in mock surrender. 'Tell me what you know.'

'While inspecting the body I came across an injection site.' Claire stretched the light and focused it on the side of the man's right leg. 'See?'

'Not really,' she admitted, after staring and seeing nothing. Then again, you'd need a magnifying glass to see an injection hole.

'Well, it's there.' Claire pointed to the outside thigh. 'I ran some blood tests and they came back positive for a potassium chloride overdose.'

'Potassium chloride?' Was she meant to know what it was? Hardly, as she hadn't studied chemistry.

'Yes, it's what's used in lethal injections in America, in those states where they still have capital punishment. Other countries, too. If there's too much potassium in the body, it sends a message to every muscle telling them to contract. Once it reaches the heart, it interferes with the balance of sodium and potassium ions. The heart then stops beating. Death is almost instantaneous.'

Whitney tensed. Not liking where this was heading.

'What you're saying is his death wasn't natural,' she confirmed.

'That's exactly what I'm saying. And without anaesthesia it would be an extremely painful way to die. When potassium chloride's injected into the vein it inflames the potassium ions in the sensory nerve fibres. In other words, the veins would burn up as the solution travels to the heart.'

Whitney shuddered. 'Could it be suicide?'

'Yes, it could be. But how likely considering he was in the middle of doing something at work? Not to mention the pain he'd have suffered. There would be easier ways to end your life.'

Another murder? On top of everything else. She rubbed her brow.

'What can you tell me about him?'

'His name is Julian Lyons. He was found dead on Saturday morning at his workplace. He was a lawyer. The coroner requested a post-mortem and his body was brought into the morgue yesterday.'

'Time of death?'

'Between eight and eleven on Saturday morning. Cause of death, heart attack. Brought on by an overdose.'

'Is potassium chloride readily available? Can anyone get hold of it?' Whitney asked.

'That's for you to find out. I believe it is, though.' Claire turned off the overhead light and covered the body with the sheet.

'Is that all the help you can give?'

'I'm a pathologist not a police officer.' Claire stalked away from the table. She was being snappier than usual.

'Is there something wrong?' Whitney hurried after her.

'Why do you ask?' Claire came to a halt and folded her arms.

'Because you seem distant. Distracted.'

'Nothing you can help me with,' the pathologist said.

'If you want to talk, you know I'm here.'

Claire paused, as if considering it, then gave a quick shake of her head.

'Thank you, but it's all under control.'

'Well, the offer's there. What other information do you have?' Whitney asked. Even though she was asking, she didn't expect anything more, or Claire would've mentioned it.

'According to the report, he'd gone into the office on Saturday as he was working on a tight deadline for some deal. He was found by a colleague.'

She'd need to get hold of that report pronto.

'And the colleague who found the body? Do we know anything about them?' She asked as she pulled out her notebook and scribbled down some details.

'I've told you everything I know. The rest is up to you.

Now, if you don't mind, I need to write up my findings. I could've waited, but I thought you'd want to know about this one as soon as possible.'

Proof, if proof was needed, that something was going on with Claire. First the mysterious phone call and now her saying she wanted to let Whitney know in advance of hearing through the usual channels. Something wasn't right.

Claire walked back into her office area, leaving Whitney to follow.

'Thanks. I'd better get in touch with George,' Whitney said, referring to the forensic psychologist who worked with her sometimes. 'She'll definitely be interested in this.'

'Off you go, then,' Claire said.

'I appreciate you calling me in on this straight away.'

'So you should. You owe me one.'

They actually owed Claire plenty. But she'd settle for one. Not that she imagined the pathologist ever calling it in. She wasn't like that.

Once Whitney had left the morgue, she stopped at the vending machine and bought herself a coffee, and then she took out her phone and hit speed dial for the forensic psychologist.

'Hello.' George answered on the third ring.

'Are you busy?' She got straight to the point, knowing George couldn't care less about engaging in small talk, despite them not having seen each other for a few weeks.

'I'm always busy.'

Between her and Claire, it was a wonder she had any self-confidence, the way they spoke to her. Although she did give as good as she got when necessary.

'Does that mean you can't get away?' she pushed.

'Why?'

'We've got a body.'

The silence hung in the air.

George let out an audible sigh. 'Not another one.'

Was her frustration due to the fact she'd have to take time away from work or because, like Whitney, the number of murders Lenchester had was staggering?

'Unfortunately, yes. How quickly can you get to the station?'

George had been having trouble at work because of the amount of time she'd been spending with the police. Whitney hoped it wouldn't affect the chance of her assisting in this case.

'Tell me more…'

'The victim is male and initially it was thought he'd died of a heart attack through natural causes. But during the post-mortem Claire found potassium chloride in his system.'

'The drug used in lethal injections?'

'Of course, you'd know that,' she said, shaking her head. 'I didn't. How quickly can you get here? I'd like your input.'

'I'll leave now and meet you at the station,' George replied, after a few moments.

Chapter Three

George pushed open the door to the incident room and was hit by the familiar sound of non-stop chatting. She enjoyed coming into the police station to see Whitney. Despite the noise, it relaxed her almost immediately. Working alone in her university office was peaceful and quiet. As much as she loved her own company, it made a pleasant change to get drawn into the excitement of what was going on here.

It would also help take her mind off what had happened between her and Ross the previous evening. It had plagued her thoughts non-stop but wasn't anything she wanted to share with Whitney. Not yet. For now, she had to process it herself and then get back to him with an answer.

She caught sight of Whitney standing by the board, talking to her detective sergeant, Matt Price. She wandered over and as she got close, Whitney looked up and smiled.

'What have I missed?' George asked.

'I was about to get Matt up to speed before delegating tasks to the team. I've just received the police report from Ellie.'

George glanced at Whitney to see her response to the older police officer's request. There always seemed to be some reason for him wanting to leave.

'What is it this time?' Whitney asked, resting her hand on her hip and tilting her head to one side.

'I've promised to take the wife shopping in the sales. She wants a new dress for her niece's wedding.'

'What time did you say you'd be home?' Whitney asked.

'No later than four-thirty.'

'What time did you get in this morning?'

'I was here at seven,' Frank said.

'Really? I didn't see you.' Whitney's eyes narrowed.

'Well, maybe it was eight.' He bowed his head, appearing suitably sheepish at being caught out.

'Why didn't you tell me you wanted to go part-time? I'd have got in touch with HR to arrange it.' Whitney glanced at George and winked.

George turned her head so Frank couldn't see her smile.

'It's just this once, promise,' Frank said.

'We've heard that before,' Doug said, shaking his head.

'Who asked you?' Frank retorted, glaring at him.

George laughed. The banter between Frank and Doug was legendary. There was nothing malicious about it as they were very close. The whole team was. She tried to imagine any of her colleagues acting like that but failed.

'Start checking the CCTV footage, and at four-thirty you can go,' Whitney said. 'But I want you in early tomorrow morning. No excuses.'

George was impressed with the way Whitney dealt with Frank. For all of his idiosyncrasies, he was a very loyal officer. Even more so since the time Whitney's daughter, Tiffany, had been kidnapped by a pair of psychotic twins.

'Thanks, guv. I'll be here by seven.'

'Good. Ellie start on the background checks. Finances. Social media. Friends. Family. Sue, you can help. Anything suspicious let me know. Doug, I want you to look into the law firm where the victim worked. We have no idea of motive, so we need to consider the possibility that it was against the firm, and not just him.'

'How was he killed?' Doug asked.

'It was a potassium chloride overdose.'

'Oh, you mean like—'

'Yes, like in lethal injections,' Whitney interrupted, deliberately speaking in a parrot tone. 'I want someone to find out how easy it is to access potassium chloride and the exact places it can be bought. According to Dr Dexter, it's readily available.'

'I'll do it, guv,' Matt said.

'Good. We'll debrief later.' Whitney turned to George. 'Are you ready to leave now?'

'Whenever you are.'

They left through the rear of the station and entered the car park.

'Your car?' Whitney said.

George stared down at her. 'Of course. It's always my car.'

'Really?' Whitney grinned. 'I hadn't noticed.'

'I've told you, there's no need to ask me every time.'

Whitney wasn't a car person and while she said she hated her old Ford, it didn't seem to stop her driving it. George, on the other hand, loved cars and anything to do with them. She'd only had her Land Rover Discovery a couple of years, but already she was thinking about changing it later in the year. She had her eye on a Porsche Cayenne Turbo S E-Hybrid in quartzite grey. It was way beyond the salary of a senior lecturer at

Lenchester University, but she had money left over from her grandmother's legacy, and she couldn't think of anything better to spend it on. She'd used her inheritance to buy her house outright and had no intention of buying anything larger as the Victorian terrace was perfect for her needs. Meaning she could spend the rest on anything she saw fit.

George hadn't mentioned the new car to Whitney. She'd leave that until she'd actually bought it, because she could imagine the comments it would elicit. Whitney had a thing about George being posh and coming from a monied background, so different from her own.

She keyed the address into the satnav, and they left. It was a crisp spring morning. The blue sky was dotted with clouds, and the air had a freshness about it. It was a time of year George particularly enjoyed, with the trees blossoming and the early flowers shooting up. They drove in companionable silence, with Whitney spending most of the time on her phone, until they reached the property.

'Wow, look at the size of that.' Whitney gave a low whistle.

'It's certainly impressive,' George agreed, nodding.

'Obviously, I'm in the wrong profession. I should have been a lawyer.'

George drove through the stone pillars and parked alongside the entrance, beside the other cars. Two Mercedes, a BMW, and a VW Beetle.

She knocked on the door and after a few minutes a man answered. Behind him were two lively golden retrievers wagging their tails and trying to push past to get to the visitors.

'Hello,' George said, patting the liveliest dog on the head.

'Is Mrs Lyons in?' Whitney asked.

'She's rather tied up at the moment,' the man said. 'Can I help? I'm her brother.'

Whitney held out her warrant card. 'I'm Detective Chief Inspector Walker and this is Dr Cavendish. We'd like to speak to her about her husband.'

A shadow crossed his face. 'It's been a very difficult time for her, but if you could wait a moment, I'll see if she's up to talking.'

He turned and left them standing on the doorstep. The dogs ran off behind him.

After several minutes, a tall slim blonde woman headed towards them. Her face, although made-up, was pale and wan.

'I'm Fiona Lyons. You wanted to see me?' Her voice was soft and there were dark smudges under her eyes, like she hadn't been sleeping.

'Hello, Mrs Lyons. I'm Detective Chief Inspector Walker and this is Dr Cavendish. We're very sorry for your loss. We'd like to have a word with you, if we may, somewhere quiet?'

'Nowhere is quiet at the moment,' Fiona Lyons said, shaking her head. 'I've got the whole family with me.'

'Are you sure you can't find somewhere? You might want to have someone with you.'

The woman frowned and gave a small sigh. 'I'll find my brother. Is it to do with Julian?'

'Yes, it is.'

They followed her into the spacious hall with a flagstone floor and cream painted walls, towards the back of the house.

'We'll go into the day room,' she said, opening a door off the hall. 'Wait here while I find my brother.'

The room was square with high ceilings and had a decorated fireplace in the centre of the far wall. On the pale, duck-egg blue painted walls were pictures of country scenes. Floral curtains hung loosely, from floor to ceiling, and large mismatched rugs covered the wooden floor.

'This is a pleasant room,' George said. 'It reminds me of my grandparents' house. I could certainly live here.'

'Me, too,' Whitney replied. 'Not that that's ever going to happen.'

They sat on one of the deep red sofas. Mrs Lyons returned with her brother following. Whitney and George both stood.

'What would you like to discuss?' Mrs Lyons asked.

'If you'd like to take a seat, please,' Whitney said.

'What is it?' the brother asked, anxiously.

He sat next to his sister, on the sofa opposite Whitney and George, and held her hand.

George stared at them, wanting to gauge their reaction when the news was broken. Knowing a death was murder changed everything.

'Mrs Lyons, the pathologist who carried out the post-mortem on your husband doesn't believe his death was as straightforward as originally thought.'

'What do you mean?' she asked, exchanging a worried glance with her brother.

'Mr Lyons' heart attack wasn't brought on by natural causes. He was found to have died of a potassium chloride overdose.'

Colour leached from the woman's face and her hand flew up to her chest. 'An overdose? He killed himself? That can't be right. Everything had been going so well for us, now.'

George's senses went on alert. What did she mean by *now*?

'It's a possibility, but at the moment we're working on the assumption that someone else administered the drug.'

Mrs Lyons collapsed in on herself. 'But why? Who would want to? I don't understand.'

Her brother put his arm around her shoulders and drew her close.

'That's what we're looking into. Would you be up to answering a few questions for us?' Whitney asked, gently.

The woman glanced up, her face tense. 'I've already done that, when the police first called here to tell me.'

'I'm sorry, but the questions I wish to ask are more related to what we now know.'

'I understand.' She nodded.

'Tell me about Mr Lyons. Julian. Did he often work long hours, or at the weekend?'

'Yes, he did. Because he worked with clients from different countries, and time zones, it wasn't unusual for him to work unsociable hours. I thought once he was made partner it would be different but, if anything, it got worse. He said he needed to keep an eye on everything.'

George leant in. That certainly wasn't the case with lawyers she knew. Being a partner may have brought with it a higher level of responsibility, but long work hours on a regular basis wasn't part of it. Hours like that were for the lower level lawyers. Much like in the medical profession.

'Do you know of anyone who might have had a grudge against Julian? Perhaps he mentioned it to you?'

'No. He'd have told me if there were issues. I don't know who his clients were, though. You'll have to speak to his colleagues about them. I can't see why anyone would wish to harm him. He was a corporate lawyer. He didn't get death threats or anything like that.'

'Mrs Lyons,' George said. 'You mentioned earlier that things were good between you *now*. Had there been some difficulties?' She sensed Whitney's eyes on her as she didn't usually speak. Her role was to watch and interpret body language.

The woman bit down on her bottom lip. 'Well…' She turned and looked at her brother, who was frowning.

'It's nothing to do with it,' he said.

'Mrs Lyons?' Whitney pushed.

'Several years ago, I had some mental health issues which affected our marriage. I withdrew from the family and spent a lot of time alone in my room. Julian tried to be there for me, but I pushed him away. I saw a psychotherapist and was prescribed medication. Now I'm fine… Julian and I had returned to how we were before, and things were good again.'

'Thank you for telling us. We appreciate your honesty,' Whitney said. 'What did Julian do in his spare time?'

'When he wasn't working, he enjoyed tennis. He played whenever he could. He also went running and to the gym. He kept himself very fit. He said he had to because with his job, he didn't want to risk burnout.'

It appeared that he hardly spent any time at home with his wife. Was it intentional?

'I understand you have two children,' Whitney said.

'Yes. Josh and Charlie.'

'Where are they now?'

'You're surely not going to speak to them,' the brother said. 'They're only thirteen and fourteen. They won't know anything because they spend most of their time at boarding school.'

'We won't speak to them now, but it's possible we may wish to in the future. Did Julian have an office at home?'

'Yes, he had his own study,' Mrs Lyons said.

'Did he spend much time in there?'

'Yes, he often worked when he was at home.'

'If you could take us, we'd like to have a look to see if there's anything that might help us with our investigation.'

They followed her out of the room, down the corridor, and into another medium-sized room. An antique desk stood near the window overlooking the garden, which seemed a little overrun with weeds and not well kept. George would have loved to get out there. Gardening was her therapy.

On the desk sat a laptop and mobile phone.

'Do these belong to Julian?' Whitney asked.

'Yes. They'd been at his office but one of his colleagues dropped them off. I didn't know what to do with them, so I put them on his desk.'

'I'd like to take them with us. They might contain information that will help our enquiries,' Whitney said.

'Yes, of course. I really can't think of any reason why someone would do this to him since he was such a wonderful husband. He always made time for the children, even though he was busy. We went on lovely family holi-days. We had an ideal life, a lovely house. He was perfect and…' Her voice broke and she let out an agonising groan.

Her brother put his arms around her. 'I think my sister's had enough. If there's anything else you need to know, please address your questions to me.'

'Mrs Lyons, where were you between the hours of eight and eleven on Saturday morning?'

'I was here.'

'Can anyone vouch for you?'

'Why are you asking?' the brother said. 'How can this be relevant? Surely you're not accusing my sister of harming her husband.'

'We just want to eliminate her from our enquiries.'

'I was alone because Julian had gone to the office.'

'What time did he leave for work?'

'I don't know. When I got up at nine, I found a note in the kitchen saying he'd gone into the office and he'd see me later.'

'Did you both go to bed at the same time on Friday?'

'I went up around eleven-thirty. I'm not sure about Julian. I took a sleeping pill so was out almost immediately. He told me he had some work to do.'

Whitney turned to the brother. 'What were you doing between the hours of eight and eleven on Saturday morning?'

'I was at home in Wales. My wife can vouch for me.'

'Thank you,' Whitney said, turning to Mrs Lyons. 'That's all we need, for now. Why don't you go and rest? We'll continue looking around the office, and then leave. I'll arrange for a family liaison officer to be with you. They'll be your link with us and the investigation.'

'Thank you,' Mrs Lyons said, sniffing.

She left with her brother and Whitney and George continued searching but found nothing obvious that would help. They left and went to the car.

'So, he's Mr Perfect,' Whitney said. 'But no one can be that perfect. The phone and laptop might give us more of an insight.'

'Yes.'

'Do you have time to come with me to Hadleigh & Partners?' Whitney asked.

George shook her head. 'No. I've got a meeting soon, which I can't miss. I'll drop you back at the station and then will have to leave.'

'Okay. Do you fancy going out for a drink later? I want to talk to you about something.' A worried expression crossed her face.

'Is anything wrong?' She could have kicked herself for

not noticing. But, as usual, things like that passed her by, especially as she had something on her mind.

She hoped it wasn't Tiffany. Whitney worried about her daughter, but judging by her social media posts and the emails she'd sent, the young woman was thriving.

'I'll tell you later. I'm trying to put it to the back of my mind. We've got to concentrate on this.'

understand from my assistant that you would like to talk about Julian.'

'Yes. Is there somewhere else we can go?' Whitney asked.

'We can stay in here,' Rupert said.

'I'd rather not as this is a possible crime scene.'

His eyes widened. 'Crime scene?'

'We'll leave this office and I'll explain,' Whitney said.

'Yes, of course.'

He led them to a small meeting room which had a modern glass and chrome circular table and matching chrome and black chairs.

'Would you like something to drink?' he offered.

'Coffee would be good,' Whitney replied, realising she'd only had two so far and she could really do with another. Her grumpiness, if she went without, was legendary.

'I'll arrange for some to be brought in.'

He left them alone for a few moments.

'Was his reaction to it being a crime scene genuine, do you think?' she asked Matt.

'I think so. Why?'

'It seemed a bit forced to me. Keep an eye on him while I ask the questions.'

'Will do, guv.'

Once Lister returned, he sat at the table next to Matt.

'During Julian's post-mortem the pathologist found his death wasn't down to natural causes as first thought,' Whitney said.

'We were told he'd died of a heart attack,' Rupert said, frowning.

'He did, but we now believe the death was suspicious.'

'How can a heart attack be anything but natural?'

'It can be brought on by many things,' Whitney said.

'And this happened at work?' His eyes widened.

'That's what we're investigating. We'd like to first interview you, and then anyone who worked closely with Julian.'

'Of course. We'll provide as much help as we can.'

She pulled out her notebook and began scribbling some notes.

'I noticed there was a second desk in his room, did someone else work in the office with him?'

'Yes,' he said nodding. 'He shared with one of our junior associates.'

'Are they in today?'

'She was, but she was very upset by his death and we suggested she went home. If we'd have known the circumstances of his death, we would have asked her to stay.'

'I'd like her details,' Whitney said.

'My PA will get them for you.'

'How long had Julian worked here?'

'He'd been with the firm for over twenty years. He began as a junior associate and worked his way up.'

'What exactly did he do?'

'He was a junior partner in the corporate department specialising in mergers and acquisitions. He mainly oversaw the drafting, reviewing, and negotiation of deal documents, from inception to completion.'

Was it more interesting than he made it sound?

'Did he ever go to court?' she asked.

'No.'

'Can you think of anyone who would have a grudge against him?'

'Absolutely not. He was well respected and liked. I can't believe anything like this could have happened.' An incredulous expression filled his eyes.

'Is it possible there's someone with a grudge against the firm?' Whitney suggested.

He rubbed his jaw. 'Of course that's possible. Anything's possible. But I can't see it, not with our type of work.'

'There must have been some grievances with clients.'

'Yes. We do sometimes have issues,' he agreed.

'We'd like a list of all clients who you've had issues with recently,' she said.

'I'll get one of the partners onto it. But I doubt there'll be more than a couple of names.'

'Would you say any of your clients skirt the law? Any who might be termed *dodgy*?' Whitney asked.

'No.' He glared at her. 'What sort of law firm do you think we are? Our clients, especially the ones Julian worked with, were respectable financial institutions, like international companies. I'm absolutely convinced it's nothing to do with the firm.'

'Did Julian often come into work on a Saturday morning?'

'No, he didn't. I was surprised to find out he'd been in, to be perfectly honest.'

Hmm…interesting. That wasn't the impression she'd got from the wife. She was convinced he worked all hours God sent.

'Not ever?'

'No. Usually, if there's any work to be done, it will be done during the week. He tended not to come in at the weekends. Very few of us do.'

'What about working late during the week? Would you say Julian worked long hours?'

'Not particularly. No longer than other partners.'

Again, interesting.

'According to his wife, he had to go in on Saturday

because he was working on something for an overseas client.'

'That's a possibility, although unlikely. Partners rarely work at weekends.'

The door opened and Rupert's PA walked in with a tray of coffees which she put down on the table.

'Thank you, Alice. I'd like you to sit down and talk to the police. It seems that Julian's death is suspicious.'

Her hand shot up to her mouth. 'You mean he was murdered?'

'We're investigating at the moment,' Whitney said, annoyed that he was trying to direct the interview.

'The police would like to speak to everyone who worked closely with Julian,' Rupert said. 'Will you be able to arrange that?'

'Yes,' she said, sitting next to him.

'Who did Julian mainly work with?' Whitney said, pen poised to write down the names.

'There's one of our junior associates who shared a room with him, but she's gone home,' Alice said.

'We'd like her contact details. Is there anyone else?'

'His secretary, Debbie,' Alice said.

'So he only worked with the junior associate and his secretary?' Whitney clarified.

'No. He worked with others, in particular Lee Peters, one of our senior associates,' Rupert said.

'We'd like to speak to Lee and Debbie.'

'I can arrange that for you,' Alice said, getting up and leaving the room.

'Do you need me any longer?' Rupert said. 'I obviously have to inform our Managing Partner about this, and the sooner the better.'

'You can go but we may wish to speak to you later. Before you do leave, please will you tell me what you were doing on Saturday, between eight and eleven in the morning?'

'Why?'

'As I'm sure you're aware, being a lawyer, we ask all people we interview their whereabouts during the time of a crime so we can eliminate them from our enquiries.'

He scowled. Was he pissed off that she'd *lawyered* him?

'I was at home in bed until eight-thirty, then after breakfast I went out shopping with my wife. After that, we went to my daughter's house to see our grandchildren.'

'And your wife and daughter can confirm that?' Whitney asked.

'Yes, of course.'

'Okay. Thank you very much.'

He left and shortly after a man who looked to be around Whitney's age walked in. He had short, dark blond hair, cut around his ears, and wore silver framed glasses.

'Hello, I'm Lee Peters.'

'Please take a seat. Have you been told by Alice why we're here?'

'Yes.' He cleared his throat. 'It was such a shock learning that Julian had died, but now we know it's a murder ...' He swallowed. 'How can I help?'

'How did you find working with Julian?'

He was silent for a few moments. 'Julian was a lovely man and he got on well with everyone. Clients and staff both liked and respected him. I can't think of anyone who would want to see him dead. It's not like he was in the public eye. He was integral to all of our deals and oversaw much of the work in the emerging markets sector. He was a hard-working family man. It's ludicrous that someone would wish to end his life.'

Could he sound any more perfect? It was a recurring theme and didn't sit right.

'Is it possible that he interrupted someone breaking in or doing something potentially damaging?' Whitney asked.

'There's nothing here of any value. Apart from our computers.'

'What about your records?' Matt asked. 'Would they be of interest to someone?'

'I suppose so. To some people. All of our files are computerised.' Lee tapped his fingers on the table.

'Who has access to these?' Whitney asked.

'It depends on what it is. Some files are password-protected.'

'Do partners have access to everything?' Matt asked.

'I assume so, but I don't see how he could have witnessed anything being taken. It doesn't make any sense.' He glanced from Whitney to Matt, a puzzled expression on his face.

'It's not out of the question,' Whitney said. 'Someone could have held a gun to his head and made him open up the computer files.'

Lee blinked. 'I hadn't thought of that.'

'In an investigation such as this, nothing is left out of the equation. What were you doing on Saturday morning?'

'I was in Bournemouth all weekend with my wife. We went to visit her family. She can vouch for me.' He let out a small sigh.

'Okay. You may go now,' Whitney said.

Lee left and before Whitney had time to discuss with Matt what he'd thought, the door opened and a woman walked in.

'Hello, I'm Debbie. Julian's secretary.' There were tear tracks down her cheeks and her eyes were red-rimmed.

'We're sorry for your loss. It must have been a big shock,' Whitney said.

'Yes, it was. I didn't find out until this morning when I

arrived at work. I can't believe it. But now I've been told you don't think it's a heart attack?'

'It was a heart attack, but it wasn't from natural causes,' Whitney corrected. 'You worked closely with Julian. What can you tell me about him?'

'He was a good boss, and everybody liked him.' She blushed slightly.

Did she have a thing for him?

'He sounds almost perfect,' Whitney said.

'No, he definitely wasn't perfect.' A shadow crossed the woman's face and she bit down on her bottom lip.

Whitney went on full alert. 'Could you elaborate on that?'

'I don't wish to speak ill of the dead,' she said hesitatingly.

'We need to find out who murdered him, and you might be able to help. That's more important than *speaking ill* of him. Tell me what you know.'

'I don't see how it can be related, because how can it be? But…' She paused. 'He did have an affair with a secretary in our property department.'

'When was this?' Whitney said.

'Sometime last year.'

'Was he seeing her up until his death?'

'No, he finished it some time ago.'

'How do you know about this and yet no one else we've spoken to has mentioned it?' Whitney was curious to know how it had remained a secret, seeing as affairs between members of the police force were seldom kept quiet.

'It's called the *secretary grapevine*,' Debbie said, making quotation marks with her fingers. 'I was told in confidence. It wasn't public knowledge. The only reason I knew was because when Julian ended it, the girl concerned confided in another secretary, who then told me.'

'Are you sure no one else knew?' Whitney pushed. She knew first-hand how quickly gossip could circulate.

'I don't know for certain, but if it had got around, then I surely would have heard about it.'

'Can you give me the name of this secretary?'

'Promise you won't say it was me who told you?' She shifted awkwardly in her seat.

Could she sound any more like a schoolgirl? This was a murder enquiry.

'We'll try not to involve you, but we do need to speak to her.'

She bowed her head. 'Okay,' she said quietly. 'Her name's Tegan Thorpe.'

Whitney wrote down the name and put an asterisk beside it. 'Where is the property department?'

'Second floor. Her desk is the first on the right as you step out of the lift.'

'Thank you. We'll go and see her now.'

Chapter Five

Whitney and Matt followed Debbie's instructions and seated at the first desk they came to was a woman who looked to be in her late twenties with straight, deep auburn hair hanging just below her shoulders. She was staring out into space, a tissue scrunched up in her hand. Her face was devoid of colour, accentuating her blood-red lips which were pressed together.

Whitney approached her. 'Hello. Are you Tegan?'

The girl started and then frowned. 'Yes.'

'I'm Detective Chief Inspector Walker and this is Detective Sergeant Price. Is there somewhere private we can talk?'

'What's this about?'

'We'd rather talk somewhere quiet,' Whitney said gently.

'Okay,' she said, shrugging. 'We can go to the staffroom.' She picked up her handbag from under the desk and headed off, with Whitney and Matt following.

After reaching the end of the large open-plan office they headed down a single flight of stairs and into an empty room facing them. There were several tables with chairs around them and a kitchen area with a fridge, microwave, dishwasher, and sink. There was also a worktop with cupboards below it.

'We can talk here,' Tegan said.

She sat at one of the tables and Whitney and Matt sat opposite.

'I understand you knew Julian Lyons,' Whitney said.

Her body stiffened. 'Everyone knew him.'

'We've been led to believe you had a relationship with him,' Whitney said, getting straight to the point.

'Who told you that?' Tegan said, her gaze darting from Whitney to Matt.

'It doesn't matter where we got our information. Please answer the question,' Whitney said, her voice firm, but kind.

She looked away and was silent for a few seconds. 'Yes.' Her voice was barely above a whisper. 'Why do you want to know about it?'

She appeared puzzled. An act?

'We've been informed by the pathologist that Julian's heart attack wasn't brought on by natural causes.'

She sat upright in her chair and stared at them. 'What do you mean?'

Whitney wished she'd brought George with her because she'd be able to tell how genuine the reaction was.

'At this point in the investigation, all we're saying is we believe his death to be suspicious and we're interviewing people at his workplace in an attempt to establish a motive behind it.'

'You think someone at work did this? You're not accusing me, are you?' Her eyes were wide.

'As I've just said, we're interviewing everyone who

came in contact with Julian. You had a relationship with him and would have known him better than most.'

'I can't see why what happened between us is relevant. It finished months ago.'

'How many months?' Whitney pushed.

'Two,' Tegan muttered.

'I'd hardly call that *months* ago. To me, that's fairly recent,' Whitney said, exchanging a glance with Matt. Was the girl trying to make her time with Lyons seem inconsequential? If so, why? 'How long were you seeing him?'

'We got together in May last year, so about eight months.'

'How did you meet?'

'I temped for him, before getting a permanent job in the property department.'

'How long have you worked here?' Whitney asked.

'Three years in July.'

'You knew each other for quite some time before your relationship began?'

'Yes.' She looked away from Whitney, her cheeks red.

'How did it start between you?'

'We had an awayday and we all went out for a drink afterwards. It developed from there. Why do you need to know? I had nothing to do with him recently.' She wrapped her arms around herself.

A barrier? Protecting herself from the questions? She'd ask George.

'How often would you see each other away from work?' Whitney asked, ignoring the question.

'Two or three times a week he'd come around to my place in the evenings. He'd tell his wife he was working late. We'd have dinner, watch television. We couldn't really go out in public in case people saw us.'

'What about the weekends? Did you ever see him then?'

'Sometimes we'd go away, if he could find an excuse. But it would have to be somewhere we didn't know anyone so there'd be no chance of being seen.' A dreamy expression crossed her face.

'When was the last time you went away together?'

'We went to Norfolk, the weekend before he finished with me.'

'Did you stay overnight on your trips away?'

'Yes.'

'How did he manage that?'

'He'd tell his wife he was going to a conference, or had to go away for a meeting. He always managed it. Not being seen or caught was important to him. To both of us. I didn't want to jeopardise my position at the firm.'

'What about his car when he came over to your place? Couldn't that have been spotted?' Whitney asked.

'He'd park on nearby streets, or get a taxi from work and leave his car in the office car park. We were very careful not to draw attention to ourselves.'

'Yet, people did know.'

Her jaw tightened. 'That was my fault. I was upset when it was over and confided in someone I clearly shouldn't have.'

'How did the relationship end?' Whitney asked.

Tegan drew in a long breath, and tears filled her eyes. 'Julian told me he was going to leave his wife and we made plans for a future together. But every time we set a date for him to tell his family, there was some reason why he couldn't do it. Something to do with the children or his wife. In the end, I gave him an ultimatum. He leaves her or we're over.'

'What was his response to that?'

'He finished with me.' A hollow laugh escaped her lips.

'Was it because of the ultimatum?'

'It must have been. He was clearly stringing me along the whole time and I was too dumb to see it.' She rested her arms on the table, her hands balled into tight fists.

Her true feelings were coming out now. But were they strong enough to kill him? Plus, why wait two months before doing it?

'How did you feel when it was over?'

'I was devastated. I couldn't eat. Couldn't sleep. Could hardly do my job. I really thought we had a future.'

'What did you say when he ended it?'

She looked away, a guilty expression on her face. 'I threatened to tell his wife all about us.'

'What was his reaction?'

'He got really angry and told me that if I did, I'd be fired and I'd never find a job anywhere else in Lenchester because he'd make sure I had a bad reference.'

A motive? Yes. But again, why the wait?

One thing was for sure, he clearly wasn't the perfect man Whitney had been led to believe.

'From what I've heard about Mr Lyons, that sounds very out of character. So far, there's been nothing but good said about him.'

'That's hardly surprising. He was an expert at getting people to like him. He would put on an act, but sometimes the cracks would show.'

'In what way?' Whitney asked.

'He could be quite moody, and always wanted his own way. Even when watching the television, he expected it to be the programmes he wanted to see.'

'What were you doing on Saturday morning?'

'I was at home until eleven, then I went into town and

did some shopping. In the afternoon I met a girlfriend and we went to the cinema.'

'What did you see?'

'The latest Marvel film.'

'Tell me, Tegan. Do you have access to potassium chloride?'

'What? No. I don't even know what it is.'

'It's not important,' Whitney said, not wanting to alert her. 'What happened after he threatened to damage your career prospects?'

'I promised not to say anything to his wife. I had no choice.' She closed her eyes for a few seconds and rocked gently.

'Was it difficult at work after you finished? Did you speak to Julian at all when you saw each other?'

'We kept out of each other's way. If I saw him in the corridor, I would just nod and say hello.'

'Did he respond?'

'He'd do the same. But that was all.' Her eyes clouded over.

Did she still feel something for him?

'Okay. We might need to speak to you again.'

'You know, I never stopped loving Julian. I might have threatened him, but that was only because my feelings for him ran so deep. I'm devastated he's dead, but I promise you, I had nothing to do with it.'

Her gut told her that was the truth, even though George would have none of it.

'Thank you for your time,' she said.

Whitney and Matt left the staffroom, but Tegan stayed seated.

'What do you think of her responses?' Matt said once they were out of earshot.

'I think we need to get back to the station and start

looking more carefully into Julian Lyons. We've got two conflicting stories about him. I suspect he wasn't the perfect colleague, husband, and father we've been told he was. Which means there may well be someone out there with sufficient motive to harm him.'

'I have to leave for our hospital appointment once we get back to the station,' Matt said.

Whitney wrinkled her nose. 'Appointment?'

'At the IVF clinic. I did mention it to you,' Matt said.

It had totally slipped her mind. She'd been too wrapped up in her mum and now the murder.

'You did. I'm sorry, I wasn't thinking. Drop me off and then I'll see you later. Good luck.'

He'd confided in her that he and his wife were trying IVF treatment. This was going to be their first appointment with the specialist.

Whitney returned to the incident room and went straight over to Ellie's desk.

'Julian Lyons' laptop and phone. I want you to have a look through his phone, using the self-service kiosk, and send the laptop to Mac in digital forensics to see what he can find.'

'Yes, guv.'

She walked over to the board and beside the photo of Julian Lyons wrote the name of his wife and the name of his mistress. Tegan Thorpe.

'Listen up, everybody. We've been to Julian Lyons' workplace, and also to his home. We're getting two differing pictures of the man. One, the perfect husband and ideal father, who everybody, including his wife, is besotted with. At his work people were singing his praises, but then we found out through the secretary grapevine that he's not as squeaky clean as we thought.'

'What's the *secretary grapevine*?' Frank asked.

'It's where they go out drinking wine,' Doug said, laughing.

'Why don't you shut up, Doug, and stop always taking the piss?' Frank snarled.

'What's got into you today? You know I love you really,' Doug said.

'Boys. Stop. Come on, let's get onto this. We've discovered he had an affair with a woman called Tegan Thorpe. He promised to tell his wife about them, and they were going to set up home together. When she put the pressure on him to follow through on their plans, he ended their relationship. It wasn't pleasant.'

'Why?' Doug asked.

'He threatened Tegan. Said she'd be sacked and would never get a job anywhere else because he'd make sure her references were bad. Not a nice guy, if she's to be believed.'

'Agreed, but do you consider that to be sufficient motive for murder?' Doug said.

'No, I don't. Mainly because all of this happened a couple of months ago. Yes, the woman is bitter, but I'm not convinced she was the person responsible for his death. What's more interesting is it has shown us there were two sides to the man.'

'Like there is to everybody,' Sue said.

'True. We need to delve deeper and find a motive. Hopefully, Ellie will find something on his phone, or Mac will retrieve something of use from the laptop. This isn't going to be straightforward at all.'

Chapter Six

George was seated at her desk, intending to do some work until it was time for the meeting, when her phone rang. She looked at the screen. Ross. Should she answer? Or just ignore him? She'd hardly had a chance to check her emails since she'd only arrived back in the office a short time ago.

More to the point, what if he wanted an answer straightaway? She hadn't had time to process it, let alone think about the implications. But she couldn't ignore him, that wouldn't be fair either.

'George speaking,' she said, wincing at how formal her voice sounded.

'It's me. Ross.'

'Yes, I know.'

'Do you have a couple of minutes for a chat?'

'I'm due in a meeting shortly, so I can't be long. Is there a problem?' Even to her ears that sounded lame. Of course, there was a problem.

'That's what I called you about. You left rather suddenly last night, and I wanted to check everything was okay.'

He'd cooked her a lovely meal and even though she hadn't intended to stay over as she wanted to be in work early and he lived quite far away, she'd planned on staying later than nine o'clock. He'd put her on the back foot, and all she'd wanted to do was escape. She wasn't proud of her behaviour.

'I remembered some preparation that needed doing for a lecture today.'

It was a total lie and he would know that. She never left anything to the last minute.

He sighed and it echoed in her ears. 'After my proposal, you clammed up. I don't want to force you into anything.'

'You're not. I need time to think about it.'

'It seemed to me the logical next step. You know I love you. And I think you feel the same way about me, even though you haven't put it into words.'

He'd told her on several occasions about his feelings. But what about hers? She hadn't actually articulated them. She found it too difficult. Did she love him?

'You know I'm very fond of you?' she said.

'Of course I do. And I know you're not open with your emotions, which is why I don't expect you to declare your undying love to me. I understand you, George.'

If he did, then he wouldn't have put her in such a difficult position. Or was she being unfair?

'Then you know how hard this is for me,' she said.

'I do. But I think you and I make a good team. Being together permanently seemed like the next step.' His voice cracked.

Had she hurt him? She didn't want to do that.

'I need time to think about it. It's a very big decision and not one I'd considered up to now. As you know, I've been in a relationship with someone before which didn't work.'

'We both have,' Ross said. 'But we shouldn't let that deter us from being happy. We make a perfect couple.'

Did they? She'd always enjoyed his company. And certainly, she felt more towards him than anyone else in the past. Stephen included.

'We do get along very well,' she acknowledged.

'I don't want you to feel I'm pushing you into anything. I'll give you as much time as you need to think it through and make a decision.'

'Thank you. I appreciate it.'

'But don't feel you have to keep away from me while you're making up your mind. I'm always here for you.'

'Yes, I understand that. I really must go now, because it's almost time for the meeting. Thank you for calling.'

She'd never been so grateful for a meeting in the past.

'When are we going to see each other next?' he asked.

'I thought we'd arranged for this weekend?'

'Great. If you want to speak to me in the meantime, you know where I am.' He gave a little laugh, but it didn't seem natural.

She ended the call and stared at the wall. What was she going to do? Had he been thinking about proposing for a while? Several months ago, he'd said he loved her and didn't seem to mind that she hadn't reciprocated. She liked him a lot. More than that. But marriage? She wasn't sure it was something she wanted to consider.

She glanced up when there was a knock on the door and her colleague, Professor Yvonne Wright, stuck her head around.

'You ready? I thought we could sit together.'

'As ready as I'll ever be.' She picked up her handbag from the back of the chair and threw it over her shoulder.

'Do you know what the meeting's about?' Yvonne asked.

'I've no idea. All I got was a text saying there'd been an emergency and a meeting had been called. Attendance compulsory. The Government hasn't released the funding figures and allocation yet, so it can't be anything to do with that. Term has already started, so it's not related to that. I couldn't think of any other possibilities.'

'Only you would start analysing in such detail,' Yvonne said laughing.

She hadn't even realised that's what she'd been doing. There was something far more pressing on her mind than sitting through an emergency staff meeting which, knowing their head of department, was likely to be something inconsequential that he'd blown up. He was that sort of man. He couldn't fight his way out of a paper bag, to quote Whitney.

'Habit,' she said.

'We'll find out soon enough. I hope it doesn't go on for too long. I want to be home on time tonight. It's our anniversary and we've booked a table at Indigo. I can already taste the lamb rogan josh I'm going to have.'

'It is the best Indian restaurant in the city,' George said. 'Happy anniversary,' she added as an afterthought.

By the time they'd reached the meeting room, most of the thirty-five members of the department were seated, talking amongst themselves. They found two chairs next to each other and after only a few more minutes, Robin Delaney, their head of department, walked in. He sat in his usual place at the head of the table where a seat had been left vacant.

'Thank you for coming in at such short notice,' he said. 'I'm sorry to tell you, I've got some rather bad news.'

That captured everybody's attention and they became silent, staring in his direction.

'Associate Professor Greg Barnes had a stroke, yesterday.' A gasp echoed around the room. 'As far as I'm aware, he's doing as well as can be expected. His wife's been in touch with us. They caught it early, before too much damage was done, but he's still going to be away from work for the foreseeable future. He's not receiving any visitors yet, but I'll let you know when he's up to seeing people.'

'Where was he when it happened?' someone called out.

'He was at home, fortunately, and his wife was there. They got him straight to the hospital. If they hadn't, he could have either died or it may have resulted in severe brain damage. I understand he's able to talk coherently.'

'The poor guy,' Yvonne said quietly to George. 'I know there's no love lost between the two of you, but even so…'

'Even so, I don't wish him any ill will,' George finished.

Others around them were muttering in pairs.

'What's going to happen to his students' work?' one of the lecturers called out.

'That's why I've called this meeting. If you can all stop talking.' He waited until there was silence. 'We'll need to reallocate his lectures and tutorials, which I'm going to be doing later and will let the relevant people know. I also need someone to step into his associate professor role on a temporary basis.'

George's ears pricked up at those words. Surely, she was the only person suitable, considering it should have been her position in the first place. He was only offered it because a few members of the interview panel disliked her working with the police.

She tensed. She thought it had stopped affecting her, but clearly it hadn't because she was still ruminating over it. But if she was to be acting AP, why hadn't Robin asked her in advance? She glanced around the room. There was no one else more qualified in terms of research, students, and tenure.

Yvonne nudged her in the side. 'Is it you?' she whispered.

She shrugged, trying to act nonplussed. 'I don't know what's going on.'

'The person we're promoting to Acting Associate Professor is Stephen Grant.'

Her heart pounded in her chest. Not Stephen. As in Stephen, her ex-partner. He might have been popular, but he was ineffective at his job. And that was putting it mildly.

She'd found that out when they were living together. He was lazy and rested on his laurels simply because he was good-looking and popular. He spent more time in the staffroom than he ever did in his office.

How the hell could he get the job that should have been given to her?

She looked up and saw him staring directly at her, a smug expression on his face. She turned away. She wasn't going to let him, or anyone else, see that she was bothered by the announcement. She had other things on her mind.

Why did everything have to happen to her at once?

'Fancy going for coffee?' Yvonne said as the meeting closed.

'Yes. Good idea.' She didn't want to be alone with her thoughts.

They headed to the university café, ordered their drinks, and found a table.

'So, what do you think?' Yvonne asked once they were seated.

'About what?'

'Stephen being acting AP. It's a bit of a turn-up for the books. I can't believe they didn't ask you.'

'You know what the general consensus is about me working with the police. That would have gone against me.

If they want to promote Stephen Grant, that's entirely up to them.' She lifted her coffee and took a sip.

'You're not bothered?' Yvonne frowned.

'Of course, I'm bothered,' she said, placing her mug on the table and staring directly at her colleague. 'But what can I do about it? I've too many other things to worry about. It's just one more thing.' Damn. She hadn't meant to say that.

'What do you mean? Do you want to talk about it?' Yvonne asked, gently.

'Not really. There's nothing anyone can do. It's something I have to sort out for myself.'

'Are you sure?'

George looked at her. She wasn't as close to Yvonne as she was to Whitney. But she didn't want to confide in Whitney because she knew exactly what her friend would say.

Maybe the view of an objective outsider would be helpful. Even though Whitney didn't know Ross very well, they'd met several times and she thought he was wonderful for George, so she wouldn't give an unbiased response to the problem.

'I've got an issue.'

'You can tell me and know it's not going to go any further.'

'You know I've been seeing Ross?'

'Yes. Your sculptor guy? When am I going to meet him?'

George frowned. Why would she be introducing Ross to her? 'He's unlikely to attend university functions because I don't. So, you're probably not.' Was explaining to Yvonne a good thing? They were only colleagues and she really didn't want to share this with anyone. 'It doesn't matter. I don't wish to talk about it.'

54

'It's up to you. I'm here if you want me.'

'Thank you.'

They finished their coffee spending the rest of the time discussing Stephen taking over from Greg. Then, she went back to her desk and stared at all the marking she had to do, wishing the assignments would somehow grade themselves, because she really couldn't face doing it. Maybe later. Except…she'd already agreed to go out with Whitney for a drink.

The question was, should she tell her about Ross? Or about Greg? Or should she not say anything because Whitney had indicated she had something on her mind she wanted to discuss?

It was all too confusing. She much preferred it when there was nothing emotional going on in her life. Did that mean she should walk away from her relationship with Ross? Why the hell he couldn't have let it stay as it was, she didn't know. Everything had been going so smoothly.

Whitney had foreseen something like that happening, but George hadn't. She'd thought he was as comfortable with their relationship as she was. But he wanted more and she didn't think she was up to it.

The way Stephen had looked at her earlier brought back all the memories of how it was when they'd lived together. She'd compromised the entire time. She couldn't get on with her work when she wanted to. He wanted to watch certain things on the television when she wanted peace and quiet.

The more she thought about it, the more she believed that changing the status of her relationship with Ross was wrong.

Okay, she'd been on holiday with him and they'd had a good time, but that was just a few days. Even though they stayed overnight with each other several nights a week, it wasn't the same as being together permanently.

She needed her space. Not to mention where would they live? There was no studio at her house, and she liked her place. It was close to work and she'd got it as she wanted. Ross would want them to live where he had his studio, which was perfectly understandable. But what would happen when she wanted to work with Whitney? The fact she was so close to the station made it much easier.

She gave a loud sigh. It was too much, and she didn't want to think about it. She picked up a student's assignment and stared at it, determined to push all thoughts of Ross, his marriage proposal, and Stephen to the back of her mind.

Chapter Seven

George parked next to Whitney and headed for the pub entrance. The St Augustus pub was one of her favourite places to visit because they sold real ale.

The pub was fairly busy, with only a few tables unoccupied and a row of people standing at the bar. She could see Whitney waiting to be served. She smiled to herself, as her friend was standing on tiptoe. It was the only way she could get noticed. Being five feet ten, George never had that issue.

As she walked over, Whitney turned and waved.

'I was going to order you a Hobgoblin as I assumed that's what you'd want,' Whitney said.

'Pint?'

'Of course. You always have a pint. I know your view on halves.' Whitney grinned and George relaxed a little. Being in Whitney's company was very easy. Most of the time.

'I'll only have one as I'm driving. But yes, that would be most satisfactory. Have you eaten?'

'Not yet.'

'Okay, let's order food as well.'

Whitney picked up two menus from the bar and handed one to George.

'I'll have the Caesar salad,' George said, after scanning what was on offer. She couldn't face anything too heavy.

'Salad? That's way too healthy for me. I'll have a bowl of wedges.'

'What a surprise,' George said, smiling for the first time that day.

'I'll wait here and you get us a table. There aren't many left,' Whitney said.

George made a beeline for one in the corner beside the roaring fire. She hung her coat on the back of the chair and waited for Whitney.

After five minutes she arrived holding a pint of beer and a glass of wine.

'Who wants to go first?' Whitney said once she'd sat down and had taken a sip of her drink.

'What do you mean?' George asked, not prepared to admit there was anything she wanted to discuss.

'There's clearly something on your mind. You weren't yourself earlier. I could tell you were distracted by some of your answers when we were discussing the case. I thought you'd like to share.' Whitney leant forward and locked eyes with her.

'It's nothing,' she replied quickly. Probably too quickly as it sounded defensive.

'Come off it, George. I know you well enough to realise when there's something going on inside that logical, no-nonsense, head of yours.'

She sighed. Maybe she would confide in Whitney. But what should she tell her? Ross's proposal. Or Stephen's promotion? Or both?

'You go first,' she said, wanting to give herself some time to make a decision.

Whitney chugged half her glass of wine and then her face twisted, as if she was in pain. 'I'm trying not to think about it. That's why I asked you to go first, because if I do, I might breakdown and totally lose it.'

George tensed. What on earth was the matter to cause this? She knew Whitney tended to get emotional, but this seemed way more serious than usual.

'Tell me,' she said gently, trying to coax it out of her.

'It's my mum.' Tears filled her eyes and she blinked them away.

'What's wrong?' George leant forward.

'They called me into the care home today because they've discovered a lump in her breast and she has to go in for some tests.' She gave a loud sniff.

Surely not something else for Whitney's mother to contend with. How would her friend cope?

'I'm so sorry. When is she scheduled to go to the hospital?'

She wanted to put her hand out and touch Whitney or give her a hug, but she just couldn't. It was too awkward.

'She's going on Wednesday, thanks to a cancellation. If not for that we'd have had to wait a couple of weeks. It hasn't been diagnosed as breast cancer yet. But it could be. It's even more worrying that they managed to fit her in sooner. If the doctor hadn't been overly concerned surely it wouldn't have happened?'

She wasn't going to tell Whitney she was probably correct in her assumption, as it wouldn't help her deal with the situation. Whitney needed support more than anything.

'Try not to think about it until you know for sure. If it

comes back positive and it's in the early stages, they should be able to do something. She'll be in the best hands.'

'I know you're right. I'm also concerned about Tiffany. I don't know whether to tell her or not.'

Whitney and Tiffany were very close and it was only natural for her to want to let her daughter know. But was that the correct thing to do at such an early stage?

'When did you last speak to her?'

'She messaged me yesterday.'

'How's she getting on?'

She'd almost come to blows with Whitney when Tiffany was deciding whether to quit university and go travelling because she'd asked George first instead of going to her mum. It took a while for Whitney and her to get back to how they'd been before. If anything, though, now Tiffany was overseas, she'd become even closer to Whitney.

'She's having a great time. The weather's fabulous, which I'm jealous about. She's having fun working in a bar and meeting lots of new people. I've been erring on the side of not telling her about Mum yet, in case it's nothing. I don't want to worry her unnecessarily and spoil everything. She'd want to return home straight away, and she's already due back in a couple of months for the twins' trial. She's being called by the prosecution to give evidence.'

It was over a year ago, when Tiffany had been kidnapped by her fellow students and friends, a pair of psychotic twins. It was the first case George had helped Whitney solve. Tiffany had been dating the male twin at the time she'd been abducted. George was nervous for Tiffany having to give evidence at the trial, especially as it would be the first time she'd faced them since her ordeal. It had taken hours of counselling for Tiffany to return to living life as she had before. George hoped it wouldn't set her back.

'That seems the right decision to make,' she agreed.

'I'll wait until we have the test results. If it does turn out to be cancer, do you think she should come home? Or stay there?' Whitney's fists were balled so tightly her knuckles were white.

'Again, until you know the prognosis, and what treatment is being proposed, you're not in a position to decide,' George said.

Whitney nodded her head vigorously. 'Plus, she'll be home soon for the trial, anyway.'

'Has she talked to you about giving evidence?'

'I've kept our discussions very light, as I don't want her to worry while she's away. When she's home, I'll go through everything in detail and talk to her about how it will all work. With my experience, I can give her a lot of advice on what it's like to take the stand and to deal with defence lawyers who try to twist your words. I'm not looking forward to her being exposed to that. I hope they won't make her relive too much of it. They're bound to use the fact she'd been dating the arsewipe murderer against her in some way.'

She had to agree with Whitney on that.

'We'll both be here to help Tiffany deal with it. And I believe you should wait until you have the full picture regarding your mother before you involve her.'

'Yes, that makes a lot of sense. I knew you'd be able to sort it out for me. You're just so logical and clear-headed. My trouble is, I get too emotional and then can't think straight, especially when it comes to family. You're right. I won't say anything until we know for sure it's serious. It could be nothing and they discover the lump is benign. There's no point in Tiffany worrying as well as me, which she would because she's so close to her granny.'

'Good. Decision made. Now tell me what's going on with the Lyons' case?'

She wanted to take Whitney's mind off her mum and didn't want to overload her with her own problems.

'We've now discovered that our perfect Mr Lyons wasn't as perfect as we first thought him.'

'That doesn't surprise me,' George said.

'Why didn't you say so before?' Whitney pressed her mouth together.

'Because I had nothing concrete to base it on and that wouldn't have helped the investigation.'

'That hasn't stopped you before,' Whitney said.

'I disagree. I like to have evidence before passing judgment. At the time, we had nothing to back up my view of Julian Lyons. It's not possible for someone to be that perfect. I suspect his wife may know more than she let on. What did you find out?'

'Your gut feeling about him was right. He'd had a long-standing affair with one of the secretaries at work and threatened her if she breathed a word about it. She'd wanted him to move in with her and he strung her along. It all blew up and he ended their relationship, warning her to keep her mouth shut.'

'I don't believe in *gut feelings*, you should know that. What's more important is that we're finding out more about him. Are we any closer to a motive? Is the woman he had an affair with involved?'

'It doesn't seem likely. The relationship ended a couple of months ago, so why wait until now? And why use potassium chloride? That's the puzzling thing.'

'It's not often a method used to murder. Which means we need to think about the actual murder itself. What message is the murderer sending? We need more bodies to establish a pattern.'

'How many times have you said that?' Whitney glowered at her. 'You're just inviting more murders.'

'Don't be ridiculous, Whitney. You have this obsession with me *jinxing* based on an illogical belief in our ability to make things happen. It doesn't work like that.'

'You're entitled to your opinion, and I'm entitled to mine.'

'Except you have no scientific evidence to back yours up,' George said.

They were interrupted by the waiter bringing their food, and they sat for a while, eating.

'Are you going to tell me what's wrong?' Whitney asked once they'd finished.

Damn. She thought Whitney had forgotten about it.

'You have enough on your plate without being bothered with my issues.' George waved her hand dismissively.

'I'm your friend. You can tell me anything, you know that, don't you? Well, you should,' Whitney said before she had a chance to answer. 'I've told you enough times.'

She had, that was true. But that didn't mean George wanted to spill everything. Having said that, she could certainly share what had happened at work and get that out of her system. It would also stop her friend from nagging her if she thought the Stephen issue was the only thing on her mind.

'Okay.' She leant forward and rested her hands on the table. 'Do you remember Stephen, who I used to live with?'

'Of course I remember him, the cheating bastard,' Whitney snarled. 'You saw him with the other woman when we were in the pub. What's he got to do with anything? I thought he was totally off your radar.'

'He's been promoted,' she said flatly.

'And?' Whitney looked puzzled.

'Remember the Associate Professor position I went for and didn't get?' Her muscles tensed just thinking about it.

'Yes.'

'The man who got it had a stroke. As a temporary measure Stephen's been promoted into his position. He's *Acting Associate Professor*.' The words stuck in her throat.

'What the... Why the hell didn't you get it?'

'That's exactly what I want to know. And half the department, if the looks on their faces when we were told were anything to go by.'

'I'm so sorry. You must be gutted?' Whitney squeezed her hand.

'You could say.'

'Is it because you're still working with me?'

Should she tell Whitney the truth? She couldn't sugar-coat it. It was what it was.

'Probably.' She shrugged. 'But that doesn't make it right.'

'I'm *so* sorry. Can you appeal the decision?'

'I doubt it. But I might take it further.'

It wasn't something she'd considered until now, but would it be worth going to the bother of doing so?

'Maybe you shouldn't do anything just yet. It's only temporary until this other guy returns to work. Often these things can come back to bite you, especially if you rile your superiors.'

For Whitney, who was known for her emotional outbursts, to suggest she erred on the side of caution, was a clear indicator that what she'd been thinking wasn't the best solution.

'Yes. But what happens if he doesn't come back, and Stephen is my permanent associate professor?' she said, finally elucidating how she felt about it. 'How am I expected to work under someone as incompetent as him?'

She hated being held hostage to her feelings. What had happened to her usual calm exterior? It was a temporary promotion and might only last a short time. And if she was honest, the added responsibility of taking on the role wasn't something she would relish. At least not until she had the Ross situation under control.

'According to you, your head of department isn't much better. So, you must be used to it. Treat this in exactly the same way.'

A shaky laugh escaped George's lips. 'You're right. I don't know why I'm letting it get to me so much. Thank you for putting me straight.'

'That's a first. Usually it's you talking me down from the ledge. Is it perhaps because there's something else on your mind?'

Or as a psychologist might say: the presenting problem isn't always the actual problem.

How perceptive of Whitney to notice.

'What makes you say that?'

'Because I know you. I'm not clairvoyant, but even I could see you were preoccupied before this Stephen stuff happened. Are you going to tell me or not? My guess is it's to do with Ross. Am I right?'

George glanced away unable to meet Whitney's eyes. 'Possibly,' she muttered.

'Come on, spill the beans. What is it?'

She turned back to face Whitney, who was staring at her with concern in her eyes.

'If I tell you, I don't want you to say anything. Just listen.'

'I promise not to say a word.' Whitney did a zip sign over her mouth.

George pressed her lips together. Asking Whitney to

refrain from talking was like asking the sun not to rise. 'Ross proposed to me.'

Whitney's jaw dropped. 'Marriage?'

'Of course. What else do you think he proposed? That we went diving with sharks? Or bungee jumping off a bridge in New Zealand? Or—'

'Don't be sarcastic, it doesn't suit you,' Whitney interrupted.

She drew in a deep breath. 'Yes, he wants us to get married. And don't act so surprised. You'd been predicting it. I'd just been too stupid to listen or notice the direction our relationship had been heading.'

'No one could call you stupid. You were too wrapped up in the rest of your life. Your work. Our murder cases. Anyway, it's amazing news and I couldn't be happier for you. What I don't get is why you think it's such an issue?'

The sixty-four thousand dollar question. And one for which the ostrich mentality was an extremely attractive proposition. Except Whitney wouldn't cease her interrogation if she chose not to think about it.

'You know me. I like my own company. My life on an even keel. I've tried living with someone. It didn't work. I'm not prepared to risk it again.' When she said it like that, it made perfect sense.

'But that someone was a shit. Ross isn't like that. You can't use your previous experience when making the decision.'

She picked up her pint and took a drink, deliberating over what Whitney had said. After a few moments of thought she spoke.

'I realise Ross is a much nicer guy than Stephen in every way possible. But, even so, my life has been going very well as it is. We see each other two or three times a week, usually staying overnight. We go away together on short breaks. Everything is perfect. Why would I wish to change it?'

'Have you explained this to him?' Whitney asked.

'No, I haven't.' She shook her head.

'Why not?'

'Because I don't know how he's going to take it. And I'm not sure how I feel about knowing he wants to get married and I don't. Maybe I should finish the relationship. That would be better all round.' She gave a half-hearted shrug.

'Before you do anything drastic, answer me this. How would you feel if you never saw Ross again?'

How could she answer that question? It made no sense. Until she experienced it, she wouldn't know.

'I have no idea. Not until the situation arises.' She sat back in the chair and folded her arms.

'Okay. Give it some thought. When did you say you'd get back to him?'

'I didn't. I told him I need some time to think about it.'

'I don't want you to make any snap decisions.' Whitney jabbed her finger in George's direction.

'I don't make *snap decisions*. I think things through. All I can see is that it's not right. I don't wish to get married. I'm happy as things are.'

'Do you think he'd be happy to carry on as you are?' Whitney asked.

Would he? It wasn't something she'd considered.

'I don't know. Why did he have to ask me and ruin everything between us? It's ridiculous. Anyway, I don't want to talk about it anymore.' She'd had enough of going backwards and forwards on this and getting nowhere.

'Before this conversation ends, answer me one thing,' Whitney said, locking eyes with her.

'What?' she strummed her fingers on the table.

'Very insightful of you. And here's me thinking you didn't have a clue as far as social cues were concerned. You've clearly been spending too much time with me.' Whitney gave a wry grin.

'You do know body language is my specialty,' George said.

'And you do know I was poking fun at you? Maybe I was wrong, you do still miss certain cues. Anyway, I was just thinking about Mum's tests tomorrow. I hope they're not going to be too painful for her.'

'The medical staff will be gentle. They're well used to doing these tests and understand how worried people are. A local anaesthetic will be used when they carry out the biopsy. You'll be able to stay with her the entire time. What time is the appointment?'

'We've got to be at the clinic late morning. After the tests I'll take her back to the care home and come into work.'

'Does Jamieson know?'

'Why?' Whitney frowned.

'I just wondered. Knowing what he's like about you and family issues.'

'I haven't told him. He doesn't need to know where I am all hours of the day.'

'I assume you'll tell Matt so he can cover for you if necessary.'

'I will. It's not like I'm going to be away for long.' She paused. 'Am I? You know about these things.'

'No it shouldn't take more than an hour.'

'Well, however long it takes, it takes. I'll deal with everything after. How are you feeling this morning?'

She certainly wasn't going to tell Whitney she'd hardly slept because of thinking about Ross and what she was going to do. Weirdly, it had taken precedence over her upset about Stephen.

'I'm fine.' She gave what she hoped was a reassuring smile.

'Had any more thoughts about Ross?'

'I'm not thinking about that now. It's put to the back of my mind. As we discussed last night, our main concern is to make some progress with the murder of Julian Lyons.'

'You're right.' Whitney banged the desk with her fist and stood up. 'Let's go and see if we've got anything from his phone or laptop yet.'

They strode out of the office, into the incident room and over to Ellie.

'What have you got from the phone?' Whitney asked.

Ellie swung around on her chair. 'Well, guv, this is interesting. There are a lot of calls between him and another number which I've traced to a Sasha Dene.'

'Who's she?'

'She works for a firm of lawyers in Lenchester. Rochester, Wilson, & Burt.'

'Is she a lawyer?'

'Yes.'

'So the calls between them could be something to do with work. What's interesting about that?' Whitney frowned.

George could tell by the smug expression on Ellie's face that she was about to pull something out of the proverbial hat. The young officer was usually self-effacing, so seeing her like this, full of confidence, was enjoyable to watch.

'An easy assumption to make. Initially I thought that until I looked at his WhatsApp account and found some extremely intimate messages and photos between them. Would you like to see?'

Within seconds a WhatsApp conversation was on her screen.

Whitney and George peered at a photograph of what looked like…

'Is that what I think it is?' Whitney asked.

'Yes,' Ellie said.

'Gross. At his age, he should know better.' Whitney screwed up her face. 'I think we can safely assume he was having a relationship with her?'

'No, they were from several months ago.'

'What about the photos on his phone?' George asked. 'Anything there?'

'I've looked at them and couldn't find anything incriminating.'

'He's obviously cleverer than that. He didn't want to leave too much evidence,' Whitney said.

'Yes, WhatsApp messages and photos are easier to delete quickly,' Ellie said.

'Except he didn't delete these, thankfully, and now we have more to go on. We need Sasha Dene's details and we'll pay her a visit.'

'Finding them now, guv.'

'When was the last time they messaged each other?' Whitney asked.

'Four weeks ago,' Ellie said.

'I wonder if they were still seeing each other, if it's been that long since they last contacted each other,' Whitney mused. 'His wife said she didn't know what time he left for work. Were there any calls or messages on his phone late Friday night or early Saturday morning?'

'No. There were no calls from the company. Actually…' The officer paused.

'What is it?'

'The absence of anything work related. This can't be

the phone he uses for work. Did his wife mention him having two phones? Companies often issue a work phone to their employees.'

'Can you find out?'

'Yes, leave it with me. I'll get onto it now. I should have thought about it sooner. Sorry.' Ellie bit down on her bottom lip.

'It's early stages, we can't think of everything straight-away,' Whitney said. 'Don't be so hard on yourself. You've done a great job.'

'Thanks, guv.'

'By the way, has anything come back from Mac yet regarding Lyons' laptop?'

'No, nothing so far. I'll give him a ring. But I don't want to be too insistent. You know what he's like if he thinks you're pressuring him.'

'I doubt whatever you say to him could be deemed pressure. You're way too nice.'

George nodded in agreement. 'In a good way,' she added, after seeing the look on Ellie's face.

'Not to mention we all know he has a soft spot for you. You speak his language... tech speak, at which I'm hope-less,' Whitney said. She then turned to George. 'Are you okay for a visit to Sasha Dene? We need to find out the exact nature of their relationship and whether she's connected at all.'

'I don't have to be back at work for a while, so I can go with you. I can probably stay away until late this afternoon.'

The longer, the better, as far as she was concerned.

'Haven't you got any lectures or tutorials?' Whitney asked, tilting her head to one side.

'I had a tutorial this morning, but don't have any lectures today.'

'Sounds like a good job, plenty of free time. How many hours do you lecture a week?' Whitney said.

'Who are you, my boss?' George snapped. 'My work comprises lecturing, tutoring, researching, being on committees, and all the admin those roles generate. I have, if you must know, five hours of lectures a week.'

'Whoa,' Whitney said, holding up her hands. 'I'm sorry. I didn't mean to upset you. It was said in fun. I know you have a very demanding job and I'm extremely grateful you can spare the time to help us.' Whitney took a step away from her.

What the hell was she doing? She was used to Whitney's humour and knew she didn't mean anything by it. She needed to stop acting like an idiot. She was surrounded by them at the university, and didn't want to turn into one herself.

'Forget it,' George said, forcing a conciliatory smile. 'I overreacted.'

'It's forgotten. Right, let's go. Actually, before we do, I want to see if there's anything on the CCTV footage around the offices on Saturday morning.'

They headed over to Frank's desk. He was facing Doug, his arms waving animatedly.

'I'm telling you now,' he said to Doug. 'If you say that one more time, I'll set him on to you.'

'What's going on?' Whitney asked, as they got up close.

'He's talking about his new dog, Butch. He's a British Bulldog,' Doug said, smirking.

George would swear the pair of them were getting worse. They weren't like that when she'd first got to know them, or was it they were no longer on their best behaviour with her around because they accepted her as one of the team? She warmed at the thought that might be the case.

'I didn't know you wanted a pet,' Whitney said. 'What will you do with it when you go on holiday?'

'The wife was desperate for a dog and now we have this lovely grey and chocolate puppy. At least, he will be lovely once he learns to do his ablutions outside and not over the new carpet. It's playing havoc with my back having to bend down all the time to clean up his mess. We might have to curtail our holidays, now. Can't say I mind. I hate flying.'

'I don't suppose Spain will mind either,' Doug said.

'Don't start, again,' Frank said looking daggers at him.

'You shouldn't have threatened me with the dog,' Doug said, glaring right back at the older officer.

'Serves you right for going on about dogs and their owners looking the same,' Frank said.

George exchanged a glance with Whitney and they both grinned. If that was the case, then yes, she could certainly see the theory being proved right. Frank was thickset, with jowls and no visible neck.

'Well, I'm sorry to interrupt this ridiculous conversation, but we have a murder to solve. Doug, I want you to go to the Lyons' house and speak to his wife. We think she may know more about her husband's adulterous behaviour than she let on to George and I when we were there. Take Sue with you.'

'Yes, guv.'

'Frank, tell me about the CCTV footage around the law firm on Saturday morning. What did you find?' Whitney asked.

Frank swung his chair around until he was facing his computer screen. He pulled up some footage.

'I went through all the cameras and didn't find anything of note. Apart from seeing the victim's car drive into the car park at eight-thirty on Saturday morning.

Here.' He pointed to the screen and they could see his car drive down the side of the building.

'His wife couldn't tell us the time he left as she woke up to find a note. Could you see anyone else in the car with him?'

'No. The camera wasn't at the right angle. They weren't well placed.'

'Damn. Were there any other cars around at the same time?'

'No. There were a couple that went into the car park later on, about nine.'

'Track them down and confirm their alibis. It was a Saturday so they would have needed a good reason for being there.'

'Yes, guv.'

'What about foot traffic? Did you see any people walking past at the time he arrived?' Whitney asked.

'Yes, from about seven onwards.'

'That's early,' Whitney said.

'There's a gym around the corner, they could be going there,' George said.

'Come to think of it, a few of them were wearing gym gear, so you're probably right,' Frank said.

'Did any of those on foot go into the office?'

'No, guv.'

'Okay, go over the footage again and double-check to see if there was anybody acting suspicious. Look for a pedestrian watching him. Anything. Go back into Friday evening, someone might have been sussing out the place.'

He gave a frustrated sigh. 'As well as tracking down alibis?'

'Yes.'

'Okay, guv. If you insist, I'll relook at the footage, but I've already looked closely and haven't seen anything.'

He was pushing his luck. Whitney was being extremely patient with him.

Whitney's jaw tightened. 'Yes, I do insist that you keep looking for our murder suspect.' She turned to George. 'Come on, let's go and visit Sasha Dene. Now we know what Lyons was like, we have more potential suspects and motives to work with.'

Chapter Nine

Whitney was silent during the drive to Rochester, Wilson, & Burt. Her mind full of competing thoughts. Her mum. The case. Whether she was losing her grip on the team.

Was she being too easy on them? Frank seemed to take advantage whenever he could.

Understandably, Matt wasn't giving one hundred per cent because of the IVF. She didn't hold that against him, but it added to the issue. She was happy for him and his wife, and hoped it would be a success, but it meant she couldn't rely on him as much, especially when it came to being her eyes and ears while she was away from the station.

On the other hand, they were loyal, and everyone pitched in when they needed to. Perhaps she was over-thinking. It wouldn't be the first time.

'Are you listening to me?' George said.

Whitney blinked. 'Yes.' She paused. 'Sorry, no. I was miles away. What did you say?'

'I asked where you want me to park as there are double yellow lines all along here.'

'Don't they have a car park?' she asked, frowning.

'Yes, but it's barrier entry and we don't have a card.'

'I don't want to draw attention by being illegally parked. Let's find a side street.'

After parking, they headed to the law firm. Whitney pushed open the glass doors and they walked in. It even smelt luxurious. 'What is it with all these law firms? No wonder they charge so much if they have to pay for the upkeep of offices like this.'

'Not all law firms are so plush. This is one of the top firms outside of London along with Hadleigh & Partners. They're competitors,' George said as they walked towards the reception.

'We'd like to speak to Sasha Dene please,' Whitney said to the receptionist.

'Who shall I say is here to see her?' he asked.

'Detective Chief Inspector Walker and Dr Cavendish from Lenchester, CID.' Whitney held out her warrant card, and he scrutinised it.

'May I ask what it's about?'

'No, you may not,' Whitney said.

What was it with people always wanting to know why they were there when it wasn't even them they wanted to speak to? Seeing her warrant card should be enough.

'Take a seat over there.' He gestured to a small waiting area where there was one other person seated, reading a magazine. Whitney and George sat in silence.

After a few minutes a tall attractive woman, wearing a fitted black skirt which ended just above her knee, and a cream long-sleeved peplum top, headed towards them. She had long auburn hair pushed off her face by a thick black headband with pearls on it.

'Interesting,' Whitney muttered.

'What?' George said, quietly.

'I believe he may have a type. Note the hair colour.'

'Noted.'

They stood as the woman strode confidently towards them.

It was like being in *Land of the Giants* standing between Sasha and George. When she was younger, she'd tried everything to grow, including putting manure in her shoes, which was what someone at school had suggested.

'I'm Sasha… you wish to speak to me?' the woman said, looking directly at George.

It was the height thing. Tall people had so much more authority.

'Yes,' Whitney said, craning her neck to make eye contact. 'I'm Detective Chief Inspector Walker and this is Dr Cavendish. Do you have somewhere private we can talk?'

'One of our meeting rooms.' Sasha turned to the receptionist. 'Brad, we're using meeting room two if anybody wants to know where I am.'

They walked down the corridor and into a small meeting room which housed an oblong table with chairs around it. In the centre was an empty jug with glasses. A large window overlooking the main high street gave the room plenty of light.

'How can I help you?' Sasha asked, after they'd all sat.

Her composure and sophistication verged on arrogance. Whitney took an instant dislike to the woman, but tried not to let it show, knowing where the conversation was heading.

'We understand you know Julian Lyons,' Whitney said.

She frowned. 'Yes. Why?'

'When was the last time you were in touch with him?'

'We haven't been in contact for a few weeks. I can't remember the exact date.' She shrugged. 'What's this all about? Please get to the point. I'm really busy and don't have time to waste.'

Whitney bristled.

'Were you having a relationship with him?' Whitney asked, softening her tone. As much as she was happy to *get to the point*, she wasn't that heartless. She was about to deliver some bad news, assuming she didn't already know.

'What's that got to do with anyone?' Sasha said, her tone cold.

'I'm sorry to have to tell you that Mr Lyons died of a heart attack on Saturday.'

Colour drained from her face. 'I hadn't heard. Why are you here?'

'Because the pathologist has informed us that his death wasn't due to natural causes.'

'Aren't all heart attacks natural causes?' Sasha frowned.

'Not always,' Whitney said.

'You think he was m-murdered?'

She slumped in her chair; her mouth open. All traces of the previous arrogance gone.

'That's what we're investigating. We have his mobile phone and found messages between you and him of an extremely personal nature. I'd like to know more about your relationship with him. When did it start? Were you still seeing him? Anything you can tell us that will assist us.'

Colour returned to Sasha's face, and she blushed. 'I've known Julian for a few years now. We worked together on deals.'

'Can you explain why you'd be working together on a deal if you're at different firms?' Whitney asked.

'It happens if we're representing opposite parties in a transaction. Depending on the deal, there are very often multiple legal teams involved from different firms.'

'How did you actually get together?' Whitney asked.

'After a particularly difficult deal, Julian suggested we go out for a celebration meal.'

'Just the two of you?'

'No. There were six of us. But once we'd eaten the two of us went on to a bar for drinks. It developed from there.'

'How long were you together?' Whitney asked.

'I suppose on and off for twelve months. I'm not sure exactly.'

Whitney glanced at George. That meant he was seeing her at the same time he was seeing Tegan from his own firm. What a bastard.

'How did the relationship end?'

'We didn't finish officially, it sort of petered out. After… There was… an incident.'

'An incident? Please explain further.'

Her nerve endings tingled. The way they always did when she was getting somewhere in an investigation. Could this be the motive?

'My boyfriend found out I was seeing Julian and he wasn't happy about it. He threatened him.'

'So, let me get this straight. You had a boyfriend, and were seeing Julian Lyons at the same time?' Whitney shook her head. The pair of them were as bad as each other.

'It wasn't serious with this boyfriend and, in actual fact, I met him after I started seeing Julian.'

'And you thought it was okay to see two men at the same time?' Whitney couldn't stop herself from blurting it out. Did fidelity count for nothing these days?

'Who are you, my mother? If I want to date two men, I will.'

She deserved that. It wasn't professional of her to pass an opinion. Even if this whole interview made her feel much older than she was.

'You were saying your relationship with Julian finished after this altercation?'

'Yes. It fizzled out from there.'

'What about your boyfriend? Are you still seeing him?'

'No, I ended it after he threatened Julian.'

'Why?'

'Because he stepped out of line and I wasn't prepared to accept it. Plus, he was getting too serious. I don't need that sort of thing in my life, I'm too busy with work.'

A disgruntled boyfriend who'd made threats. Could he be the one?

'What's his name?' Whitney pulled out her notebook from her pocket and began to scribble some notes.

'Lewis Evans.'

'How did he take you ending the relationship?' she asked looking up from her note taking.

'Not good.' Sasha shook her head.

'What did he say exactly?'

Sasha averted her gaze. Maybe she did have a conscience. 'He blamed it on Julian and said if I hadn't been seeing him, we would still be together. But there's no way Lewis would have done anything to harm Julian. He's not that sort of person,' she said defensively.

'What do you mean, *that sort of person?*' Whitney asked.

'Lewis was kind and he cared for me a lot.'

'How did Lewis find out about you and Julian?'

'He got hold of my phone and read the messages between us. Then he followed me one evening when I told him I was working late. The next day he confronted me.'

'And you admitted it?' Whitney asked.

'Of course, I did.' She sat upright in her seat. Clearly she wasn't suffering from guilt at her deception.

'How soon after the discovery did Lewis threaten Julian?'

'The next day.'

'What happened?'

'Lewis waited for Julian to leave work and accosted him. They were both fit men and worked out. But Julian also did weights, so he would have been stronger than Lewis if it had turned physical. He told Lewis where to go. I don't think it got violent.'

'How do you know?'

'One of them would have told me. If it was Julian who'd *won*, he would have bragged about it. If it was Lewis, he'd have been mortified at what he'd done. Neither of those things happened.'

'Do you have Lewis's details?' Sasha pulled out her phone and called out a number and address which Whitney wrote down. 'Where does he work?'

'He's a self-employed IT consultant. He works three days a week for Lenchester Hospital.'

Would that give him ready access to potassium chloride? Something else to investigate. She looked at George, who was nodding. She must have had the same thought.

'Do you know which days?' Whitney asked.

'Monday, Wednesday, and Friday.'

Which meant they might find him at home today.

'What were you doing on Saturday, between eight and eleven in the morning?' Whitney asked.

'I was at my flat.'

'Was anybody with you?'

'No. I was on my own. I got up around nine, had breakfast and watched some morning TV. After that I cleared out my wardrobe and did some washing.'

'Did you go out at all?'

'No. I read in the afternoon, ordered pizza for dinner, and then binged on Netflix. A very uneventful day.'

It surprised Whitney. She would have imagined the woman having a much more exciting private life.

'Did you speak to anyone during the day?'

'In the morning, around nine-thirty my mother called. We chatted for half an hour.'

'Anyone else?' George asked after a few seconds silence.

Whitney tossed a grateful glance in her direction. At the mention of Sasha's mother her mind drifted to her own and she hadn't thought to ask the follow-up question.

'Other than that, no. Apart from the pizza delivery guy.' Sasha looked at her watch. 'I have a meeting soon that I can't get out of. Do you need me for anything else? I've told you everything I know.'

'That will be all for the time being. We may be in touch again, if we need more information.'

Sasha escorted them back to the reception, and they left the building.

'Next stop, Lewis Evans,' George said, once they were outside.

'Definitely. Thanks for stepping in with the question. I'm struggling to focus at the moment because of Mum. I think I'm okay then out of the blue it hits me. The mention of Sasha's mother did it to me this time.'

'I understand. It's a worrying time for you. But I'm here.'

'Thank you.' She flashed George a grateful smile. 'Come on. Let's go. This lead could turn out to be the one to wrap up the case.'

Chapter Ten

Lewis Evans lived in an old three-storey Victorian terrace in Lenchester, next door to a house George had nearly bought, before settling on her final choice.

As they walked up the short path, George cringed at how overgrown the front garden was. That sort of negligence frustrated her. It wasn't as though it was a large space. It would only take an hour or so to tidy it up. Her fingers itched to be the person to do the job.

Whitney knocked on the door. There was no answer, so she knocked again. Eventually the door opened and a man appeared. He was over six feet tall, toned, chiseled features, with blond hair and warm blue eyes. There was something kind about his face.

Plenty of murderers had *kind* faces.

'Lewis Evans?' Whitney asked.

'Yes,' he said.

'I'm Detective Chief Inspector Walker and this is Dr Cavendish. We've come to speak to you regarding your relationship with Sasha Dene.'

'Why, has something happened?' he asked, panic etched across his face.

'Sasha's fine. If we could please come in, we'd like to talk to you inside.'

He opened the door and led them in to the open-plan living area, decorated in creams with chrome and glass furniture. It had obviously been renovated. Although it was spacious, the attempt to give it a modern feel meant the Victorian vibe was completely lost. George much preferred her house which, though updated, still retained the ambience appropriate to the time in which it was built.

'We can talk over here,' he said, leading them into the kitchen area and gesturing for them to sit on the stools lining the breakfast bar, while he stood beside the fridge opposite.

'Nice house,' Whitney said.

'Thank you. I've just finished doing it up. I did most of it myself.'

Yet, couldn't go that one last step and complete the garden.

'An IT consultant who's also a DIY expert. Very impressive,' Whitney said.

George looked at Whitney and frowned. It wasn't that out of the ordinary. Or was she wanting to put him at his ease?

'I learnt from my father. I'm sorry to hurry you, but what's this about? I'm trying to prepare for a conference. I'm one of the presenters.'

'Where's the conference?' Whitney asked.

'London. I'm leaving this evening and return on Friday.'

'I understand you know Julian Lyons.'

A dark shadow, crossed his face. 'Why?' His body tensed and he folded his arms tightly across his chest.

Definitely defensive behaviour.

'How well did you know him?' Whitney asked.

'He had a relationship with my girlfriend and I found out about it. We're not close friends.'

'We understand you threatened him,' Whitney said.

His cheeks went pink. 'What anyone would do in my situation? Why are you asking?'

'But she'd been seeing him before she was seeing you,' Whitney continued, not answering his question.

'When Sasha and I got together, she told me about him, but I thought it was over. She didn't give me cause to think it was continuing. I found out she was still seeing him and saw red.'

'How did you find out?'

He averted his eyes. Classic avoidance.

'Did you check her phone?' George asked, forcing his hand.

'She'd left her phone on the side and I looked. I shouldn't have done it. I saw messages between the two of them.'

'You knew her passcode?' Whitney said.

'I'd seen her unlock her phone often enough. I knew the pattern, without knowing the actual numbers.'

'Walk me through exactly what you did once you saw the conversations between Sasha and Julian Lyons,' Whitney said.

He leant against the fridge and rubbed his brow. 'I confronted her, and she admitted it, but she said it wasn't serious. I've never been so angry. Hurt and angry. I wanted to have it out with him, so I caught him after work.'

'What happened during this altercation?'

'It didn't turn into a fight, if that's what you're thinking. I'm not a fighting person. I just warned him to stay away.'

'What did Julian Lyons say once you'd accosted him?'

'He told me to back off, or I'd be sorry.'

'He threatened you physically?'

'It was all bluff. But I wasn't prepared to risk it, so I walked away.'

'What happened between you and Sasha after this?'

'It became strained. I wanted to take things further and have her move in, but she didn't want to.' He bowed his head.

Did he still have feelings for her?

'Then she end the relationship?' Whitney asked.

'Is that what she told you?'

'Yes.' Whitney nodded.

'She said she wasn't in the right headspace to move in with me. Whatever that meant,' he said in a monotone voice.

'Which is what you were looking for?' Whitney confirmed.

'Yes. As I've already told you.'

'After her refusal what did you do?'

George leant forward. The situation wasn't dissimilar to her and Ross. Could their situation be resolved? If this was anything to go by, then no. It couldn't. Both parties in a relationship should be at the same point.

'When she said she didn't want to move in, I was happy for us to continue seeing each other. I didn't want to end it altogether. But she decided it was over because she didn't think I'd be content with our relationship carrying on as it was.'

'Was she right, do you think?' Whitney asked.

'Look. I'd rather have been with her than without her. If that was what she wanted, I would have gone along with it. What's this all about?'

'How early?' Whitney pushed.

'Sevenish.'

'It's hardly light at that time,' Whitney said.

'It's light enough.'

'Were you anywhere near Hadleigh & Partners during your cycle ride?' Whitney asked.

'Possibly, but I didn't have anything to do with the death of Julian Lyons. I keep telling you.' He shifted awkwardly from foot to foot.

'Get your jacket, you're coming to the station with us for questioning.'

'A-are you arresting me?'

'We'd rather you came with us of your own accord, so it's entirely up to you. We'll be sending someone to search your house. With your permission, of course.'

'Do I have a choice?' He looked from Whitney to George.

'Yes. But if you refuse, we'll think you have something to hide,' Whitney said.

'I want a lawyer present at my interview,' he said.

'Do you have one?' Whitney asked.

'My friend's a lawyer, I'll call him.'

'Okay. We can wait.'

He picked up his phone and headed to the far side of the room; the lounge area. They couldn't hear exactly what he was saying, but after a few minutes he headed back over to them.

'He's meeting us there in an hour. How long will I be at the station? I have a lot to do. I haven't packed yet.'

'As long as it takes,' Whitney said.

George smiled to herself. Whitney was skilled at not taking shit from anyone. Never done rudely, but with enough authority that the recipient knew who controlled the situation.

'Why don't I meet you at the station as I have preparation to do for the conference.'

Was it true or did he want time to hide evidence? He'd certainly mentioned this *preparation* enough. She imagined Whitney was already onto that.

'We'll stay here with you until my team arrives. Then we can leave together. Do you have the conference details?'

He picked up his phone from the side and unlocked it. He showed them details of an IT conference being held in the centre of London. His name was listed as one of the presenters.

They arrived back at the incident room and headed over to Ellie. Whitney showed her the pills. 'How's your research going regarding potassium chloride? We found these in Lewis Evans' cupboard. Could they have been turned into liquid for injecting into our victim?'

She couldn't see how, but she wasn't a chemist.

'You can buy liquid potassium chloride online, guv. It's very easy to get hold of. I doubt Evans would have been able to extract liquid from the tablets.'

'Are there any restrictions on the amount purchased?' she asked.

'The quantity needed to produce a heart attack isn't huge. Not enough to send warning signals to companies selling it,' Ellie said.

'Can you find out whether Lewis Evans bought any?'

'I'll see what I can discover. His credit card receipts will help.'

'Let's see what the search turns up. Matt should be there by now.'

They'd remained at Evans' house until Matt and Sue

had arrived to do the search and then returned to the station with their suspect, who was waiting in one of the interview rooms for his legal representative to arrive. After the solicitor called to say he'd been delayed, she'd come back upstairs with George.

'How long can you stay?' she asked George. 'We've no idea when the solicitor will be here.'

George looked at her watch. 'I've got another hour.'

'Okay. We'll—' her mobile ringing interrupted her. She held it up to her ear. 'Walker.'

'We've gone through the house and found nothing, guv,' Matt said.

'That was quick,' Whitney said.

'The place is immaculate. It's clean, tidy, and he didn't have too much to look through. He's into healthy living, but no liquid potassium.'

'Was there any liquid stored that you couldn't identify?' she asked, thinking he could have put it into an unmarked bottle.

'No. Nothing.'

'Okay. Come back to the station.' She ended the call. 'That was Matt. They've done an initial search and found nothing. I'm going to let Lewis Evans go. For now. I don't want to take up valuable time interviewing him at this stage. That doesn't mean he's off our radar, though.'

They needed more evidence if he was to be incriminated and she wasn't convinced they were going to get it.

Whitney phoned down to the front desk and instructed the officer on duty to go to the interview room where they'd left Evans and inform him he could leave.

Chapter Eleven

'Was it worth it?' I ask my reflection.

My lifeless eyes stare back at me. Offering no answer to my question.

What did I expect? That suddenly life was going to be worth living again? How could it?

Nothing I do will change what happened in the past. Nothing is ever going to make me feel whole.

Apart from if I was dead.

Then the numbness would stop.

Then I wouldn't be able to look back at things with regret.

Then…

But I'm not dead. And nor will I be for a long time, unless fate steps in and gives me some release from this hell I'm living.

I could end things myself. But that would be the coward's way out. I can't do that. Not to your memory.

Shall I stop, then?

No.

Just because killing didn't ease my pain, doesn't mean they should live when they don't deserve to, after what they've done.

That's not fair.

They need to know they can't get away with what they've done.
That's not how it works.
Actions have consequences.
Death is theirs.
They will learn. I will force them to.
My verdict is final.
Your death won't be in vain.
They will pay. Forever.

Chapter Twelve

Whitney hurried into the entrance of Cumberland Court. She was running late as the day's briefing had overrun. Then Jamieson had caught her, wanting to know where they were on the case. They couldn't be late for the appointment in case they lost their allocated time and ended up missing out. The thought of having to wait any longer filled her with angst.

She quickly signed in and made her way upstairs to her mum's room. Hopefully the tests wouldn't take too long, as she wanted to get back before Jamieson noticed she was absent. Matt knew where she was and she'd instructed him to say she'd gone out to visit a possible suspect. If pushed, he'd tell Jamieson he wasn't sure who it was. She doubted the Super would ask for a name, though. He'd never done so in the past. He believed them to be inconsequential details that shouldn't be run past him. Occasionally, his predictability was a plus.

Whitney walked into her mum's room, expecting to see her seated and ready to go. But she was still in her night-dress, sitting in the easy chair by the window. Whitney looked at the bed and saw her mum's clothes lying in a heap on there. She must have got herself undressed.

'Mum. Why aren't you ready?' she exclaimed. 'Our appointment's in an hour, and we've got to get across the city.'

'Where are we going?' her mum asked, frowning. 'No one told me.'

'We're going to the hospital for tests.'

Of all days for her not to be with it, today wasn't one of them.

'What tests?'

'Don't you remember? They found a lump in your breast and they're going to examine it today to make sure there's nothing untoward going on.'

'What lump? I want my breakfast.'

She sucked in a calming breath. The one thing she'd learnt was she had to stay relaxed when her mum was like this, otherwise she'd get even more disorientated and upset.

'You had your breakfast earlier. Come on, let's get you dressed. It looks like you've taken your clothes off and put on your nightdress.'

'It's time for bed. I'm tired. I stayed up late last night.'

'Did you? What did you stay up late for?'

'I was watching something on the television.'

'What was it?'

'An old episode of *Morse*.'

'Did you enjoy it?'

'Did I enjoy what?' Her mum frowned.

Whitney's insides clenched. '*Morse*.'

'I don't know what you're talking about.'

'I need to get you ready. We're going to the breast clinic. Do you want me to help you?'

Whitney picked up the dress from the bed and went over to her mum, who was staring out of the window.

'Come on, Mum, let's get you dressed and ready.'

'Ready for what? Why are you here?' her mum said in the same vague voice. Whitney took another calming breath and held up the floral dress.

'I'm here because we're going to the clinic at the hospital.'

'What hospital?'

Whitney tensed and forced back the tears which were threatening to fall. She hated to see her mum like this, but she knew it was to do with her condition.

'I'll tell you what, I'll go downstairs to find Angela.'

If she brought her mum's favourite carer, that might help. She ran downstairs. As luck would have it, Angela was sitting on reception with one of the other members of staff.

'I've just been to see Mum to take her for the tests, but she'd put her nightdress back on and now won't get dressed.'

'Oh, did she? I didn't think she was having such a good day today.' Angela's face filled with sympathy.

'Can you help me?' Whitney glanced at her watch. They'd end up being late at this rate and lose their appointment.

'Yes, of course. Come on. We'll go and sort her out together.'

They went upstairs, and into the room. Her mum had taken off her nightdress and was pulling on her dress over her underwear.

'Hello, Whitney. I'm nearly ready.'

Whitney exchanged glances with Angela. Obviously her mum had flit back into understanding what was going on. Thank goodness.

'That's great, Mum. Let's brush your hair and then we can go.'

They managed to leave within ten minutes and Whitney drove them to the hospital. On arrival at the breast clinic, they were ushered to a lovely waiting room, unlike the usual hospital areas Whitney had been in. There were comfortable easy chairs, carpet on the floor, and artwork on the walls. Whitney was handed a questionnaire to complete.

'You'll have to help me with this,' she said to her mum. 'Is there any history of breast problems in the family?'

'Not that I recall.'

'Okay, I'll put no. Do you have breast implants?' She glanced at her mum and they burst out laughing.

'Not something I've ever needed,' her mum said, grinning and sticking her chest out.

'You'll like this next question. Are you on the contraceptive pill?'

'Why are they asking? Of course I'm not.' Her mum tutted.

She was glad they'd refused to have a carer accompany them. Having this time alone with her mum when she was totally with it was something she cherished and didn't want to share with anyone.

'Are you on HRT?' Whitney smirked.

'No. Not that either.'

Whitney finished the questionnaire and took it to the nurse on reception, who explained how the appointment was going to go. She returned to her mum, who was reading a magazine.

'Mum, first of all they're going to give you a mammogram and then an ultrasound. After that they'll decide if you need a core biopsy.'

'What's that?' her mum asked.

'They put a very fine needle into the lump and take some cells so they can assess them. It's all done under local anaesthetic, which will numb the area, so you won't feel anything. The results of the mammogram and ultrasound are immediate. If they do the biopsy, then we'll have to wait a week before they can tell us what they've found. What they find will determine what, if any, treatment you need. Do you understand?' Her mum appeared to be listening, but she wanted to check.

'Of course, I understand, Whitney. I know all about this.'

She glanced up to see a nurse heading in their direction.

'Mrs Walker?' the nurse asked her mum.

'Yes.'

'Please come with me.'

'I want my daughter to stay with me.'

'That's perfectly fine,' the nurse said.

After the mammogram and ultrasound, it was decided to do the biopsy. Whitney stayed the entire time, impressed with how well her mum coped. Even regular mammograms could feel invasive.

After the tests they left the hospital, and her mum seemed in good spirits.

'Can we stop somewhere for a coffee? I haven't been out for ages,' her mum asked.

Whitney glanced at her watch. Another half hour wouldn't make a difference, especially if her mum wanted to discuss any possible procedures and needed reassurance.

'That would be lovely.'

She chose a small café close to the hospital and ordered coffee and cake for them both. Whitney allowed her eyes to close for a second as she drifted back to the past. To a time when they'd go out, just the two of them, if Whitney wasn't on duty, and Tiffany was at school. Her dad would take care of Rob. They called it their *special time.* That all ended once her dad died.

'How's Tiffany getting on?' her mum asked, pulling her back from her memories.

She forced a smile. Her mum had clearly forgotten she'd asked the same question a couple of days ago. 'She's having a great time. She's working in a bar with her friend Phoebe and they're enjoying themselves in the sunshine. I envy her being in the warm. I'd love to wear T-shirts all year round.'

'Do you speak to her often?'

She was lucky Tiffany did keep in contact. She knew people at work whose kids had gone overseas and they were lucky to hear from them once a month.

'Yes. She texts most days and we speak once a week.'

'I'd like to talk to her. Can you arrange it? I'm sure Rob would, too.'

'Tiffany would love that. I've just about got to grips with the time difference between England and Australia. I'll bring Rob over to you early one morning, when it's evening for Tiffany and we can have a WhatsApp conversation.' She was sure the assisted living home her brother lived in wouldn't mind him having an early breakfast.

'Thanks, love.'

Whitney stared at her mum, grateful for these moments they could still share together. It was something she could no longer take for granted.

The waiter came over with their order and placed it in front of them, the smell of the coffee invading her senses. She was in need of this caffeine fix, that was for sure.

'How's work going?' her mum asked, after taking a bite of her cake.

'You know, the usual. There's always something occupying my time.'

'More murders?'

Her mum's usual question. Hardly surprising seeing as Lenchester was fast giving *Midsomer Murders* a run for its money.

'As it happens, yes I'm working on one.'

'Tell me about it.' Her mum had a fascination with Whitney's work, going back years to when she first joined the force. In another universe she might have joined up herself. But Rob's situation prevented that.

'There's not much I can tell you, other than a lawyer from one of the big Lenchester firms has been killed. Initially it looked like natural causes because he'd had a heart attack. After the post-mortem it was discovered that he'd been injected with a lethal dose of potassium chloride.'

'Isn't that what they use in—'

'Yes.' She interrupted before her mum could finish. 'That's the drug.'

'Just the one murder?'

'Yes. And I'm hoping it will remain that way.'

'You've dealt with a lot of serial killers recently, so let's hope this isn't one of them.'

'Mum!' she exclaimed.

'What?'

'You're jinxing.'

'Sorry.' Her mum grinned. 'Hopefully this time it didn't work.'

'I'll second that.'

'I'd better let you get going, then. Do you want to take me home now?' Her mum picked up her cup and finished her coffee.

'I don't want to rush you.'

'You're not. When will I see you next?'

'As soon as I can, and I'll bring Rob with me. Hopefully

we'll have your test results next week and that will put our minds at rest.'

'We've got to be realistic, love, and prepare ourselves for it being something we don't wish to hear.' Her mum rested her hand on Whitney's.

Whitney blinked away the tears. 'I know. But we've also got to remain positive. Come on. Let's go.'

She took her mum back and hurried to work, glad of the distraction because she couldn't bear the thought of her mum having breast cancer. Not that on top of everything else. How would she cope?

Chapter Thirteen

'Walker,' Whitney said as she answered her phone, the call interrupting the briefing she'd convened the following morning to discuss their progress with the case.

'It's Claire,' the pathologist said abruptly in her ear.

What did she want? Hadn't they discussed everything to do with Julian Lyons? They weren't due to receive any more information from her. The report had already arrived and it hadn't told them anything they didn't already know.

'Hello.'

'I thought you'd like to know I've got a body here with exactly the same signs as the previous one.'

'Heart attack?' She stiffened.

'Of course, heart attack. We haven't been in touch this week regarding any other person have we?'

That was snappy, even for Claire. Was she okay? Difficult to tell. Maybe she'd been called out early in the morning? That always wound the pathologist up.

'What can you tell me about the victim?'

'Initial inspection revealed a fit, healthy young woman.

She was found dead in the gym changing room earlier today. The body's here at the morgue and I've begun my post-mortem. It appears she had a heart attack. I found an injection site in the leg, which is why I called you. I thought it might aid the investigation if you knew immediately. I'll be sending her bloods to toxicology for confirmation.'

'Do you believe it to be another potassium chloride overdose?'

'I'm not prepared to pre-empt the findings.'

'But you must suspect it, or you wouldn't have contacted me.'

'Obviously.' Claire gave an impatient sigh which echoed in her ear.

Another body. Her mum had been right. She was like a magnet to them.

'Do you have the name of the deceased?' she asked.

'Carly Connor.'

'Which gym was it?' Whitney asked.

'Fitness for Women. It's on Deacon Street.'

Whitney's heart pounded. That was around the corner from Hadleigh & Partners. Was there a connection?

'Okay, thanks. I'll look into it. I want to check whether she worked at the same firm as the other victim, as it's located close by. I'll be in touch later.' She returned her mobile to her pocket. 'Listen up everyone,' she said, calling the team to attention. 'We have another victim. Her name is Carly Connor and she was found at a gym close to Julian Lyons' office.'

'Here we go again.' Frank groaned. 'The media will have a field day. We're already known as *Serial Killer Central*.'

'Two victims don't constitute a serial killer. You should know that,' Doug said.

'Try telling that to the press.'

'Whatever it is, we need to solve it. Ellie, find out if she worked at Hadleigh & Partners. Text me as soon as you have any details. I'm going to the crime scene. Doug, arrange for scenes of crime officers to meet me there. I'll report back later.'

She returned to her office to collect her belongings and straight away phoned George.

'Hi, Whitney.'

'Are you at work?'

'Where else would I be?'

'Can you get away?' Her jaw tightened with impatience. 'We've got another body.'

'What can you tell me?'

'We don't know much, other than she was found dead at the gym this morning. I've just had a call from Claire. She suspects a heart attack, and she's found an injection site. I want to take a look around the scene. Can you meet me there?'

'Yes. Give me twenty minutes.'

'It's the women-only gym on Deacon Street, around the corner from Hadleigh & Partners. I'll see you there shortly.'

The gym was situated between two shops. The frontage was blacked-out glass so it was impossible to see in. She walked through the double doors. A number of women were milling around in their gym gear. Her brows knitted. Why hadn't they closed the place?

She went to the front of the queue at the reception desk.

'I'd like to speak to the manager,' she said to the woman, holding out her warrant card. 'Detective Chief

Inspector Walker. It's regarding the death of one of your members this morning.'

A collective gasp went up behind her. Clearly they hadn't been informed of the situation. Whitney turned to face the women. 'Please wait on the other side of reception until I've finished talking.'

'I've got to get to work. I don't have time to wait,' one of the women said, her hand on one hip staring at Whitney.

'What do you want?' She glared at the woman. Someone was dead and all she could think about was herself.

'To arrange a personal training session.'

'I'm sure you can phone or ask another time,' Whitney replied.

The woman stomped off, muttering under her breath and the others moved to the side.

'It was so awful,' the receptionist said, bringing her hand up to her chest. 'I couldn't believe it. Carly was a regular here and she was always very nice to me. Thank goodness it wasn't me who found her. I don't think I'd have coped. I've never seen a dead body before. I—'

'What's your name?' Whitney interrupted, anxious to get a word in.

'Sharon,' the young receptionist replied.

'I know this has been a shock, but I'd like to ask you some questions. Are you up to it?'

'Yes,' she replied, nodding.

'Whereabouts was Carly found?'

'In one of the changing rooms.' Sharon pointed down the corridor.

'Was Carly found before or after she'd been in the gym?'

'After. She came in early, around six, as usual, and did her workout. She was found later.'

'Has the changing room been closed?' If it hadn't their crime scene would be toast.

'Yes, it has.'

Whitney breathed a sigh of relief. Thank goodness for that. 'Find the manager and ask her to meet me in there. Where is it?'

'Walk to the end of the corridor and it's the third changing room on the right,' Sharon said.

Whitney turned as the front door opened and George entered. She waved her over, ignoring the group of scowling women who were still gathered by the vending machine.

'I'm just about to go to the changing room where the body was found,' she told George. She turned back to Sharon. 'Who found Carly?'

'One of our cleaners.'

'Is she still here?' Whitney assumed they wouldn't have a male cleaner in a women-only gym.

'I'm not sure. She was very upset and Dee, our manager told her to rest in the staffroom.'

'What time was Carly found?'

'About seven-thirty this morning.'

Whitney glanced at her watch. It was already nine-thirty. Damn. The forensics would most likely be shot with everyone going about their normal business. Although if the changing room was closed, then hopefully there wouldn't be too many compromises.

'Were you on duty then?'

'Yes, I've been here since we opened.'

'I want the rest of the gym closed for the day because this could be a crime scene.'

The girl's jaw dropped. 'But I thought she just died from a heart attack or something? T-that's what Dee said.'

'It's not been confirmed. I want you to ask everyone to leave. Unless they were here at the time of the death.'

'Everyone has gone, who was here earlier when Carly was found.'

'I want names and contact details of all staff and customers who were around at the time of the death.'

'I'll have to speak to Dee. I'm not authorised to do that.'

'Don't worry. I'll speak to her about it. Do you have CCTV?'

'Yes,' she said.

'I want yesterday and today's footage emailed to this address.' Whitney took out a card and handed it to her.

'I'm not sure if I'm allowed to do that either.' Sharon bit down on her bottom lip.

'I'll clear it with Dee, too. Contact her now and ask her to meet me in the changing room.'

She sighed. Why couldn't people just do as she'd asked instead of putting obstacles in the way?

'You were a bit short with her, weren't you?' George said as they walked away from the reception desk.

Whitney glanced at George, taken aback. For her to mention it meant she must have come across as being really off.

'Was I? It wasn't intentional. I guess I'm on a short fuse.'

'Your mother?'

'Yes. She had her tests yesterday, and now we've got to wait for the results. It's going to be the longest week in history.'

Her body trembled. What if it was cancer? Everything would change. How would her mum cope? How would she cope? And Tiffany and Rob? A cloud of despair enveloped her.

'How's your mother holding up?'

George's question drew her away from her thoughts.

'She's fine. Sometimes she's like she used to be. Other times she isn't. That's the problem. You never know when you visit what she's going to be like.'

'I'm sorry. It must be tough for you.'

'Yes, but I'll get through it. How's it going for you at work with *you-know-who* in charge?'

'I haven't had anything to do with him, so far. I've made sure to keep out of his way. At least now the pitying stares have stopped. People are leaving me alone to get on with my job. So, in actual fact, not a lot has changed.'

'What about the guy who's off? Is he going to be away for a long time?'

'I've no idea. I haven't enquired. I don't intend to visit him, it's not like we were close colleagues. My priority is to keep out of Stephen's way, and for him to keep out of mine.'

They walked into the changing room, and Whitney pulled on her disposable gloves. Where was the body found? It wasn't obvious. She looked around. There was nothing which struck her as out of the ordinary.

'Hello.' A tall woman, in gym gear, with dark hair tied up into a bun on top of her head was standing in the doorway. 'I'm Dee, the manager.'

'Detective Chief Inspector Walker and Dr Cavendish. We're here regarding the death of Carly Connor this morning,' Whitney explained. Not that it was needed.

'Yes, it was a shock. My first dead body. It does happen in gyms but this was the first time for us.'

Whitney drew in a breath, before delivering the news. 'We have reason to believe Carly's death was suspicious.'

'Murder?' Dee grabbed the side of the lockers running along one of the walls.

'That's what we're investigating at the moment, having spoken to the pathologist. The gym is to be closed for the rest of the day, at least. I need the scenes of crime officers to have full access to all areas. I also want to know how many staff were on duty when Carly was here.'

'Apart from me, there were two instructors, plus Sharon our trainee, and our cleaner Jeri.'

'What were the rest of the staff doing when this happened?'

'I was taking an aerobics class. There were two girls in the gym helping our clients, and Sharon was sitting on reception.'

'Is Jeri still here?'

'Yes. I said she could leave, but she didn't want to. Her children are at school and she couldn't face being alone at home. She's still in the staffroom, too upset to continue her work.'

'Who did finish the cleaning?' Whitney asked, conscious of crime scene contamination.

'No one. I was going to wait until tomorrow morning for the changing area and showers in here to be done. Jeri had already done the rest.'

'I'll speak to her shortly. You didn't think to close the gym after Carly was found?'

Surely they would have protocols in place to deal with situations like this? One of them being to close the gym. If for no other reason than out of respect for the deceased. Unless profits came first. It wouldn't be the first time she'd encountered that.

'We kept everybody out of the way until after the police and ambulance had left with Carly. Other than that,

I didn't think it was necessary. The police officers didn't tell me to.'

Understandable, if they thought the death wasn't suspicious.

'Have you contacted head office to let them know what had happened?'

'Not yet. It's on my list of jobs to do.'

'They need to know. Especially as we're now investigating the death. Who is your immediate boss?'

'I have an area manager who lives in Birmingham and is in charge of all the gyms from Nottingham down to Watford. I'll inform him of what's happened once we've finished here.'

'I've asked Sharon for the CCTV footage to be emailed to me. I'm assuming that's not going to be an issue?'

'No, of course not. I'll make sure it gets sent immediately. Anything we can do to help.'

'Did you see anybody suspicious hanging around this morning?'

'Not that I noticed. It's quite busy first thing, because people come in before they go to work.'

'How many customers would you say you had in today?'

'Maybe twenty.'

'Did you know them all?'

'Some by name. Some by sight. They would've had to swipe themselves in, though. They would all have been members.'

'Can anyone get in without using the swipe?'

Could the killer be a member of the gym?

'If it's the actual gym then no, because the door only opens with a swipe card. The swipe then activates that person's account. They have to swipe to use the equipment, too. It saves members having to complete record cards of what they've done. The system does it for them.'

'What about the changing rooms? Is it possible someone could have gone in there without signing in?'

Dee gave a slow nod. 'It is possible, I suppose, if there are a few people hanging around, someone could slip past reception without being noticed.'

'Do you ever have any men coming in here?' George asked.

'Sometimes. A plumber or electrician. Also, the equipment is serviced by men.'

'Were any in today?' Whitney asked.

'Not to my knowledge. You'll need to check the CCTV footage, and sign-in book, to make sure.'

Did that mean their murderer was a woman? It was certainly something to consider.

'Does the camera pick up everyone who heads towards the changing rooms?' Whitney asked.

'It depends on where the person was situated. If they kept close to the wall, then it's likely the camera may have missed them.'

'We'll have to look at the footage,' Whitney said. 'Is it usual for someone to be alone in one of the changing rooms at such a busy time?'

'She was found in changing room three, which is furthest away from reception and gets used least. That could be the reason.'

'Why is it used least?'

'The showers aren't as powerful as in the other two, so our members gravitate towards one and two. It's mainly new members who use three.'

'Which Carly isn't. So why did she use it today?'

'I don't know.' Dee shrugged.

'When she was found, was she still in her gym gear or had she already showered and changed?'

'She was in her work clothes.'

Whitney walked over to the bank of three showers. The curtains were open, and she peered in. They didn't appear to have been used. There were no soapsuds, or water dripping. She'd confirm with SOCO once they'd done their work.

'Maybe she used her usual changing room and then was called into changing room three to help someone?' Whitney mused, more to herself than Dee.

'I don't know,' Dee answered.

'The gym needs to be closed straight away,' Whitney reminded her. 'I'll let you know when you can reopen.'

'I understand. I'll get in touch with my manager and let him know.'

'We're going to interview Jeri now.'

'I'll take you to her,' Dee said.

They followed her to a large room situated behind the reception. It had a kitchenette containing a microwave, fridge, and a small hob. In the corner sat a woman who looked to be in her thirties, reading a magazine. She glanced up.

'Do you want me to leave?' she asked, looking at Dee and then Whitney and George.

'No, Jeri. This is Detective Chief Inspector Walker and Dr Cavendish. They'd like to speak to you about this morning.'

The woman bit down on her bottom lip. 'Urm… okay. Why?'

'We're investigating the death, as it might not have been from natural causes,' Whitney said.

'Would you like me to stay?' Dee asked.

'We'll take it from here,' Whitney said. 'When my officers arrive, they'll want to speak to all the staff. Make sure they don't leave once the gym is closed.'

'Okay,' Dee said as she turned and left them.

Whitney and George headed to where Jeri was sitting and pulled around a couple of chairs so they were facing her.

'I know you've had a shock, Jeri, but it would be very helpful if you could answer some questions for us,' Whitney said, kindly.

'Yes.' Jeri nodded.

'Have you worked at the gym for long?' She always started gently, to put the person at their ease.

'About eighteen months.'

'Do you always work early in the morning?'

'Yes. My shift starts at six.'

'Dee mentioned you didn't want to go home and be alone in the house. She said your children are at school.'

'Yes, that's right.'

'How old are they?'

'My son's eight and my daughter's six.'

'Who takes them to school when you're here?'

'My husband gets them up and gives them breakfast. He then drops them off at school on his way to work.'

'Where does he work?'

'He's a health and safety adviser at Arkott, the biscuit factory.' She frowned. 'But he has nothing to do with this,' she added.

'We're just trying to get a full picture. Please could you run through exactly what happened this morning,' Whitney asked.

She clasped the gold chain around her wrist between her thumb and forefinger. 'I cleaned the gym and the reception area first, as always. Then I went to the changing rooms. The first two I did, no problem, but I went into the third and straight away I saw…I saw…' Jeri brought her hand to her chest as if trying to catch her breath. 'On the floor. She… she…'

'Take it slowly,' Whitney said. 'You're doing very well.'

Jeri gave a loud sniff. 'She was lying on the floor, staring at the ceiling.'

'How was she positioned?'

'On her back with her arms by her side.'

'Was the shower running?' Whitney asked.

'No.'

'What about her personal items? Were they with her?'

Jeri grimaced. 'I don't know. I didn't see. I'm sorry. It was such a shock. I…' Tears filled her eyes and she blinked them away.

'How did you react when you saw Carly?' Whitney asked.

'I stepped closer. Her face was grey and her eyes blank.'

'Did you realise she was dead?'

'I wasn't sure, but I thought she might be. It was her eyes which did it.' She grimaced.

'What did you do next?'

'I ran out and called for help. Dee came in and took over from there.'

'While you were cleaning, did you notice anyone acting suspiciously? Someone who you thought shouldn't have been there.'

'No, I didn't. I don't know who the members are. When I'm cleaning, I keep my head down. I don't want to interfere with people working out. I'm really sorry.'

'No need to apologise. Thank you for your help. We'll leave you here.'

They left the staffroom and Whitney pulled out her phone and called Matt.

'I'm having the gym's CCTV footage sent to my email

address. I'll forward it to you once it arrives. Get Frank onto it straightaway. Cross-check with the footage from Lyons' office to see if there are any similarities in respect of cars and people. What has Ellie found out so far?'

'The latest victim works at Hadleigh & Partners, as their human resources director.'

Whitney let out a sharp breath and George gave an enquiring glance.

'She worked at Hadleigh's,' she explained in a soft voice. 'Thanks, Matt. I want you to organise some officers to come here pronto to interview the staff. I thought SOCO were on their way.'

'They should be there soon. There are some traffic hold-ups because of an accident.'

'Okay. We'll wait for them to arrive and then head over to the law firm. I don't know yet if they've been made aware of the victim's death. We'll sort that out once we get there.'

'Okay, guv. I'll see you later.'

She turned to George, who was frowning. 'What's on your mind?'

'I've been deliberating on the means and motive. It's a very interesting way to murder. Why potassium chloride? What does it signify? Also, the motive appears to involve the company. It's too much of a coincidence not to be, and we don't believe in those. But—'

'We need more bodies,' Whitney said, interrupting her.

George glanced at her. 'Obviously now we have a second body it helps, but we do need more. Lewis Evans can't be our killer. He's away at a conference.'

'So he said. But we'll check to make sure he's actually there.'

'We also need to consider that our murderer could be a woman.'

Chapter Fourteen

George waited while Whitney spoke to the interviewing officers and also to SOCO, and then they left for the law firm. As it was only around the corner they walked. Whitney was still being quiet and abrupt, and most unlike her usual self. Ironically, it helped George push her own problems to one side. Neither of them could do their job if they weren't one hundred per cent focused.

They entered Hadleigh & Partners and headed for the reception desk.

'Hello, Detective Chief Inspector,' Chelsea, the receptionist said.

'We'd like to speak to whoever's in charge.'

'In charge of which department?' Chelsea frowned.

'Overall in charge of the company,' she said.

'Amelia Harte is our managing partner.'

'Is she in today?' Whitney asked.

'Yes, she is.'

'We'd like to speak to her straight away. We'll be over there.' Whitney pointed to the waiting area.

After a short time, a young man walked towards them.

'Detective Chief Inspector?' he asked, looking at George.

'No, I'm Dr Cavendish. This is the Detective Chief Inspector.' George gestured to Whitney.

'I'm Amelia's executive assistant. Would you come with me, please?'

They took the lift to the top floor and he took them to a corner office. He knocked on the door and opened it, gesturing for them to walk in. As they entered a woman who looked to be in her late forties stood. She had dark blonde hair, cut into a long bob which ended just above her shoulders.

'Good morning, I'm Amelia Harte. Is this about Julian? Such a dreadful thing to happen.'

'We'd like to talk to you about Carly Connor, your HR director. Shall we sit here?' Whitney gestured to the round table in the corner of the office.

'Carly?' She cocked her head in confusion before seeming to recall her manners. She coughed. 'Yes, of course,' she said heading around her desk and coming to sit opposite George. 'What about her?'

'We weren't sure whether you'd been informed yet, but we're sorry to have to tell you, she was found at the Fitness for Women gym this morning, having had what appeared to be a heart attack.'

Amelia stiffened. 'Is she dead?'

'Yes. We've since heard from the pathologist that it most likely wasn't brought on by natural causes, so we're treating it as a suspicious death.'

'The same as Julian,' the woman muttered, the colour leeching from her face.

'Unfortunately, yes,' Whitney said.

Silence filled the room and the seconds ticked on before Amelia finally spoke.

'We have now two members of staff who have been murdered. What the hell is going on?'

'We need to interview all members of staff who worked with Carly. What can you tell me about her?'

'Carly had been with us a number of years. Maybe six or seven. She started off as an HR manager and then got promoted to director eighteen months ago.'

'What did her job involve?'

'She would oversee all the HR functions in the company. Training and development, employee relations, succession planning, salary and benefits, and communications.'

'Did she have any contact with clients?'

'No, her role was inward facing. There was no need for her to deal with them.'

'Can you think of anything she'd been involved in recently which might have caused any problems?'

'All companies have staffing issues from time to time, and we're no different. But nothing has happened which would result in her being murdered.'

'What about her connection with Julian Lyons? Did they work together?' Whitney asked.

Amelia paused for a moment. 'Not as such, but they were both on the committee designing the new appraisal system.'

The appraisal system. George remembered the hassle caused when the university implemented a new one. But as to it being the cause of the victim's murder, she doubted it.

'Was this fairly recently?' Whitney asked.

'They began meeting six months ago, and the new system is being put in place with the round of appraisals starting next month. Surely, you can't believe this anything to do with the deaths? It's nonsensical.'

Whitney didn't answer the question, she just tapped her pen against her notebook.

'Who else was on the committee with them?'

'There was a junior associate from the banking and finance department, a senior associate from litigation, and an admin officer from commercial. We wanted to make sure most areas were represented.'

'Any other HR members?' Whitney asked.

'Yes, one of our managers,' she said.

'We'd like to speak to everyone on the committee. We'll start with the person from the HR department.'

'I feel that I ought to break the news to them first, if that's okay? I'll come with you.'

They went with Amelia and took the lift down to the floor below.

'This is the HR department,' she said, as they stepped out. 'Carly's second in command, Geraint Jones, will need to take over. We'll tell him first.'

They headed to an office with a glass window in which there was a man peering at his computer screen.

Amelia knocked on the door and opened it. He did a double take when he saw them and immediately sat upright. George closed the door behind them.

'Geraint, this is Detective Chief Inspector Walker and Dr Cavendish. I'm afraid we have had some bad news regarding Carly. This morning she had a heart attack and died.'

He gasped. 'Oh, my God!'

George scrutinised his face, looking for any telltale signs of prior knowledge of Carly's death. There were none.

'It's being treated as a suspicious death.'

'What? Not another one.'

'We'd like to look in Carly's office,' Whitney said.

'I'll leave you with Geraint,' Amelia said. 'I need to contact the partners and let them know, so they can inform their teams. I'll personally tell the others on the appraisal committee.'

'We'll be interviewing everyone who works here. My officers will be here soon.'

Amelia left the room, and Geraint took Whitney and George to the office belonging to Carly. It was adjacent to his only much bigger. The sign *Human Resources Director* was on the door. On the desk were photos, and a computer; and on the walls were certificates of Carly's qualifications.

'How long have you been working here?' Whitney asked.

'About ten years,' he said, voice shaking. The news had clearly upset him.

'Before Carly started?'

'Yes, that's right.'

'But she became director over you.'

'We both applied for the position, but I didn't get it.' He pressed his lips together in a thin line.

He certainly harboured resentment over that.

'How did you feel when that happened?' Whitney asked.

'Unhappy. But there was no bad blood between us. Carly was more qualified than me. That's why she was promoted.'

Good answer. But that wasn't how he felt, judging by his lack of blinking while answering.

'In what way was she better qualified?' George asked.

'She had broader experience. I joined the firm as soon as I'd left university and then studied for my HR qualification in the evenings. This is the only company I've worked at, whereas Carly had positions in several business environments before she joined us.'

'Did you work well together?' Whitney asked.

'Yes, we did.'

'Were there things you would've done differently had you been in charge?' George asked.

'Maybe. But that's true of anyone, in any position.'

'Did you have anything to do with Julian Lyons?' Whitney asked.

'No more than any of our employees.'

'He was on the appraisal committee and you weren't. Did you mind?' Whitney asked.

'Not at all. My main responsibility is employment contracts, so it doesn't fall under my remit.'

'Thank you for your time. Before you go, can you think of anyone who had an axe to grind against Carly?'

'She could be quite abrasive, but she didn't fall out with people. I'm absolutely stunned that this has happened. I'll have to tell the rest of the team.'

'Double-check with Amelia that it's okay. Although as we'll be speaking to members of the department, it makes sense that you should.'

'I'll speak to her now,' he said.

'Did Carly have an assistant?'

'Yes, she did. Lizzie.'

'We'd like to speak to her. Do you have a meeting room on this floor?'

'Yes, it's left out of here and the last room on the right.'

'Take her there. We won't be long. Don't mention anything about Carly, we'll tell her ourselves.'

He left them in the room, and they spent a few more minutes looking around and checking in her desk, but there wasn't anything of note. They left for the meeting room. When they got there, a woman was standing by the window looking out.

'Lizzie?' Whitney said, as they entered.

'Yes.'

'I'm Detective Chief Inspector Walker and this is Dr Cavendish. We'd like to talk to you. Please take a seat.' Whitney gestured to the chairs around the table.

They all sat down.

'What is it?'

'I'm very sorry to tell you that Carly died earlier this morning.'

The girl's jaw dropped. 'Died? What happened?'

'She was at the gym this morning and suffered what appeared to be a heart attack. Although we are treating her death as suspicious.'

'This is the same as Julian,' Lizzie said, looking from Whitney to George.

'You know Julian?' Whitney said.

'Of course, he's a partner. I know all of them.'

'Did you have anything to do with him on a regular basis?'

'Not usually, but he was on the appraisal committee with Carly, and I would prepare documents for them. This is awful. Two people dead.'

'Can you think of anybody who has a grudge against Carly?'

She paused for a moment. 'A grudge? No. No one. She was well liked at the company.'

'I understand she could be quite abrasive,' Whitney said.

'It depends on who you ask. She liked to get things done and providing you did your work properly there wasn't a problem. But there are always going to be some people who aren't happy with what we do. Especially if they'd been disciplined, dismissed, or made redundant.'

'Can you think of anybody let go recently who might have an issue with the company, especially Carly?'

'Not off the top of my head. Even though Carly oversaw everything that went on in the department, we have specialist managers to look after staffing issues. I still can't believe I won't see her again.' Her eyes were clear, no grief evident.

Was she genuinely upset?

'Did you and Carly always see eye to eye?' George asked.

Lizzie coloured. 'Not always. But that doesn't mean I wanted to see her dead,' she added quickly before taking a deep breath. 'I've been looking for another job.'

'Thank you for your honesty. What time did you arrive at work today?'

'At eight-thirty.'

'Where were you before then?'

'At home with my boyfriend. We drove into the city together. He works close by. He dropped me off. I don't know what to do now,' she said.

'Wait for Geraint. He's going to be informing the rest of the staff. Here's my card. If you can think of anything else that might help, don't hesitate to get in touch.'

'Thank you. I will. But there's nothing. Why would anyone want to kill two people from here? We're just a law firm in Lenchester. This is crazy. It's what you see on TV, not in real life.'

George met Whitney's eyes. She could say that again.

Chapter Fifteen

'Listen up, everyone,' Whitney said as they walked into the incident room. George followed her over to the board. 'We now have two bodies, both of whom died of heart attacks, and worked at Hadleigh & Partners.' She wrote that up on the board and also pinned up a photograph of Carly. 'Apart from working for the same company, the only connection between the two, that we can find so far, is they were on a committee who were tasked with designing a new appraisal system.'

'I can't see that being anything to do with it,' Frank said. 'Who cares about appraisals?'

'Some people do. Because it's where people set targets, which go towards promotion,' George said.

'That's me ruled out,' Frank said. 'There are only a couple more years before I retire, and I'm certainly not progressing higher than DC.'

'We know that,' Doug said, laughing. 'But there are others who actually take appraisal seriously.'

'Really? I doubt it. It's just another bit of paper-pushing they get us all to do,' Frank said.

Even though Whitney had viewed it in very similar terms in the past, she certainly wasn't going to admit it.

'We're not here to discuss the merits of having an appraisal system. Matt, have uniform finished the interviews at the gym?'

'They're on their way back now. I'll check in with them and see what they've got for us.'

'What about the CCTV footage? Were any men there this morning?'

'No, guv,' Frank said.

'Did you see anyone heading towards changing room three? It's the last one as you go past the reception.'

'No guv, it really only focused on the main reception area.'

'Okay. I'm going to hand over to George now to talk through what we know so far and how it can help.'

George stepped forward. 'We can't deduce too much because we only have two bodies, but the law firm is the likely connection. Also, injecting the victims using potassium chloride is quite a risky thing to do because they could be seen, or overpowered. It's very hard to approach someone and inject them.'

'So why do it?' Frank asked.

'It's most likely symbolic.'

'An execution?' Doug asked.

'That's a possibility. But as yet we have nothing to confirm it. We need to consider that the murderer was known to both victims. Julian Lyons went to his office on a Saturday morning, which he usually wouldn't. Had he arranged to meet the killer? Did they orchestrate the meeting? If not, how did they know he'd be there?'

'How easy would that have been?' Matt asked.

'We don't know,' Whitney said.

'What about this second victim?' Frank asked.

'We know she visited the gym regularly, and it wouldn't have taken long for the murderer to ascertain that, if they'd been following her. At the moment, I'm not prepared to give any sort of profile on the type of person to do this, as it would involve guesswork. But I will say that it's pointing to the offender being female.'

'We need more bodies,' Frank said.

'Correct. With that, I'll hand you back to Whitney,'

'Thanks, George. Has anyone got anything else to tell me from their research so far? Ellie?'

'Carly Connor lives in Lenchester with her partner Brent Yates.'

'Has he been informed?'

'According to the database, yes. Two PCs called to see him earlier.'

'We'll need to speak to him. Anything else?'

'I found nothing untoward in her finances. Her social media presence is fairly limited.'

'Any link between her and Mrs Lyons?'

'Not that I've come across, but I'll continue looking,' Ellie said.

'Did you check whether Lewis Evans did actually go to his conference in London?' Whitney asked.

'Yes, guv. He was there the entire time,' Ellie said.

'Doug. Did your interview with Mrs Lyons come up with anything?'

'We broached the subject of his affair, and she acted shocked, but whether it was genuine, I don't know. Now we have the second body, it would put her out of the frame.'

'Possibly, but we won't discount her involvement yet. I need to see Jamieson. He'll no doubt have something to say about what's happened so far. What are you doing now, George?'

'I'm going back to work. I've got a lecture at three and I want to do some additional preparation.'

'Okay. I'll keep in touch. What about tomorrow? Can you spare some time? We need to go back to the firm to interview any staff who worked closely with our victims. I'd like you with me to observe their reactions.'

'Give me a ring and we'll see.'

George left and Whitney headed up to see Jamieson. She walked along the corridor and could hear him talking on the phone. She waited for him to finish, knocked on the partially open door, and walked in.

'Hello, sir. I've come to tell you there's been a second death from the same law firm.'

'What's the name of the firm?'

'Hadleigh & Partners.'

He frowned. 'That's my law firm. We need to solve these murders asap.'

'We're working hard on the case. As yet, we have no motive. Our first victim was a partner, Julian Lyons, and the second, Carly Connor, the HR Director. It does indicate the company is involved, because we've found no other connection between the victims than that. They were working together on the same project: a new appraisal system. We also know that Lyons had affairs. We've already spoken to two ex-girlfriends.'

'Might there be more?'

A serial adulterer? She wouldn't be surprised.

'We haven't found any yet, but we're investigating.'

'Could he have been involved with the HR director?'

'We'll check. I'm here because we need to discuss the press conference.'

'Leave that with me. I'll arrange it and let you know.'

'Mid-afternoon would be a good time if we can fix it that soon,' she said, as she turned to leave.

She returned to the incident room and went over to Ellie. 'Text me Carly Connor's address. Matt,' she shouted. 'Stop what you're doing. I want you to come with me to visit the latest victim's partner.'

'I'll be with you in a sec, guv.'

They drove to a pretty village on the outskirts of Lenchester and pulled up outside a small cottage with a thatched roof. The door was answered by a man with red-rimmed eyes whose face was ashen. His dark hair stuck out in all directions, as if he'd just got up from his bed.

'Are you Brent Yates?' Whitney asked, gently.

'Yes.'

'I'm Detective Chief Inspector Walker and this is Detective Sergeant Price. We'd like to talk to you about Carly.'

He opened the door and led them into a small sitting room. Two floral chairs and a sofa were centered around a black fireplace. There were pictures on the mantelpiece of him with Carly, both holding a set of skis and smiling.

Whitney's insides clenched. Visiting grieving people was the worst part of her job.

Especially, as she now had to tell him Carly's death was potentially a murder.

'I'm very sorry for your loss,' she said.

'I don't understand it. She was so fit and healthy. How could she have had a heart attack? It makes no sense. She ate well. She exercised. She did everything right. It's not like she was overweight and spent her time blobbing out in front of the TV.' He rested his head in his hands.

'This is what we've come to talk to you about. We've

heard from the pathologist and we're now treating Carly's death as suspicious.'

He shot upright and stared at her, his eyes open wide. 'What do you mean?'

'We believe Carly might have been given an overdose of potassium chloride, which induced a heart attack. The pathologist is waiting for confirmation from the toxicology lab, but that's what it appears to be.'

They were going to be announcing how the murder was carried out at the press conference soon, so she didn't believe it to be an issue for him to be told.

'Murder? Why? Who?'

'That is what we're investigating. Did she tell you that Julian Lyons, one of the partners, died on Saturday at his desk?'

'Yes. It was a difficult situation for her to deal with. She was putting together a counselling package for those who knew him.'

'Is that what they usually do if someone at the firm dies?' Matt asked.

'No. But because he died at his desk, she thought it was something they should offer their employees.'

'Initially it was thought Julian died from a heart attack due to natural causes, but it's now believed his death was suspicious, too,' Whitney said.

'Also potassium chloride?' he asked.

'Yes.'

'Were they killed by the same person?'

'That's the theory we're working on. Can you think of anyone who might have had a grudge against Carly? Or anything that had happened at work which caused her problems.'

'No, not at all,' he said, running his fingers through his

hair. 'He was a lawyer and she worked in HR. Their paths seldom crossed.'

'I understand they were working on the appraisal committee together?'

'Oh, yes, she did mention something about it. Surely that wouldn't cause any issues.'

'We're investigating all possibilities. Can you tell me what you were doing on Saturday first thing in the morning, from eight, and early this morning after Carly left for the gym?'

'Why?' he looked puzzled.

'So we can eliminate you from our enquiries.'

'On Saturday we went to London for the day. We left at seven and caught the train at eight. We went shopping in the morning and took in a show in the afternoon. *Everybody's Talking About Jamie.* We were home by eight. Today, I was here when Carly left for the gym. We'd arranged to go out for dinner tonight. The police came around to tell me what had happened before I'd left for work. She…' his voice broke, and a single tear ran down his cheek, dropping onto his shirt.

'Would you like a cup of tea?' Matt asked.

He shook his head.

Whitney waited while he drew in a breath and appeared more in control.

'Did Carly drive to the gym this morning?'

'Yes.' He nodded. 'She always does… did.'

'Did she have a set routine?'

He nodded. 'She would leave here at five-fifteen, park in the office car park and go to the gym from there. She'd work out for an hour or so and be at her desk around seven-thirty.'

'How many days a week would she do this?'

'Four, but it depended on what else she'd got on. Sometimes they'd have breakfast meetings, so she'd go straight to work.' He paused. 'Oh…' His mouth opened slightly, and he stared at her.

'Yes?'

'I've just remembered something. I'm not sure if it's relevant, and you might already know. Some time ago, there was a complaint made against Julian Lyons. I don't know who, but it was one of the firm's clients. Carly wasn't happy about his behaviour, but I believe she managed to sort it out.'

Whitney's ears pricked. 'Do you know what the complaint was about?'

'No. She didn't tell me, and I didn't pursue it. She's privy to all sorts of confidential information, and I wouldn't put her in a difficult position by asking. The only thing she did say was she was disgusted by his behaviour and would rather he got his comeuppance but, as the firm had to come first, it was her job to make it go away. Really, she shouldn't have told me that much.'

Whitney drew in a breath. This was just the sort of information they needed. She'd follow it up with Geraint when she was next at the law firm.

'Thank you, that's very useful. If you do think of anything else that might help the investigation, please contact me.' She handed him a card and he stared at it, turning it over and over in his hand.

'I can't believe anyone would want to murder Carly. It's so… so… what am I going to do now? We were due to go on holiday in two weeks. I'll have to cancel it,' he said muttering to himself, as if oblivious to their presence.

'Is there anyone we can call, someone who can be with you, rather than being on your own?' Matt asked.

'My parents live on the south coast. So, no. I'll be fine on my own.'

'Have you told them?' Whitney asked, assuming they'd want to help their son with his grief if they could.

'Not yet.'

'Would you like us to do that for you?'

'No. Thank you. I'd rather deal with this on my own.' He stood and led them to the front door.

'What do you think?' Matt asked as they got into the car.

'I think we now have something solid to investigate. I'll go with George tomorrow and investigate this alleged complaint.'

The drive to the station took twenty minutes and as they walked back into the incident room, Doug called out, 'Guv, there's a message for you from the Super. He's arranged the press conference for three-thirty. He said for you to meet him at his office and you'll go down together.'

'Okay, thanks, Doug.'

She glanced at her watch. That left precisely ten minutes. On the way, she stopped at the bathroom, brushed her hair and reapplied her lip gloss. She then headed to Jamieson's office.

She knocked on the door and walked in as he was buttoning his jacket.

'Come in, Walker,' he said with a beaming smile on his face.

She did a double take. What the hell was going on? He appeared in an unusually good mood.

'Yes, sir. Are you ready to go?'

'I am indeed. Is there anything else you have to tell me?'

'We've been to see the partner of our second victim and he mentioned an issue the victim had to deal with on behalf of Julian Lyons. We're going to investigate that in the morning.'

'That's excellent. Well done.'

She wanted to pinch herself. He'd never been like this before. Had she stepped into an alternate universe?

'Thank you, sir.'

'I've got something to tell you, but I don't expect you to breathe a word of this to anyone.'

Now he was back to normal.

'Sir, you know anything you tell me is in confidence, if you ask for it to be.'

'Good. A few moments ago the news came through that I'm down to the last two in the position I've applied for.'

Whitney couldn't help a big smile crossing her face. If he got the job her life would be so much easier.

'That's excellent. I'm so pleased for you. This is the job working at the Met for the government isn't it?' she clarified.

'That's the one.'

'When will you find out?'

'They're conducting final interviews next week, so I'm hoping very soon. I won't be available on Tuesday, but I'm sure you'll manage without me.'

'Yes, sir.'

'Come on then, let's go,' he said.

They headed to the conference room in companionable silence. Actually, he glided rather than walked. Whitney could hardly contain her own excitement. With a bit of luck, he'd soon be gone.

Melissa from PR was waiting for them and she led them into the room. After introducing them, she passed the mic over to Jamieson. She glanced at him. He really needed to take that smile off his face because they were reporting murders.

'Thank you for coming in to see us. We have to inform

you that we're dealing with two suspected murders. Both victims worked at the law firm Hadleigh & Partners.'

'How were they murdered?' one of the reporters shouted.

'They were both given injections that induced heart attacks.'

She glanced at him. How come he was answering all the questions and not passing them onto her?

'As in lethal injections?' somebody else called out.

Whitney rolled her eyes, if she heard that one more time, she was going to scream.

'Yes,' Jamieson said.

'Who are the victims?'

'We're not releasing the names yet out of deference to their families, but we would like anyone who believes they have information relating to the crimes to please contact us.'

The conference continued with Jamieson fielding all of the questions and, once finished, they left the room.

'I'll see you later, Walker,' he said, as they parted company at the stairs, and he marched off.

Chapter Sixteen

George pulled on her coat and threw her bag over her shoulder, delighted to have the opportunity to leave work and go with Whitney to the law firm. The issue with Ross still weighed heavily on her mind, and it frustrated her that it seemed to be invading everything she did. It didn't help that she was still annoyed over Stephen being promoted, despite assuring anyone who asked her that she wasn't at all bothered.

She opened her door and, in her peripheral vision, spied Stephen heading in the direction of her office. She pretended not to have noticed him and hurried towards the door leading outside into the university grounds, having no intention of finding out whether he wanted to speak to her.

When she arrived at the station, Whitney was already waiting in the car park. She pulled up beside her and rolled down the window.

'Hop in,' she said.

They headed into the city centre, slowing the car as they joined the long tail of traffic. There were cones everywhere and large signs warning of expected delays. Whitney tapped her fingers against her knee.

'Have you thought any more about the proposal?' Whitney asked.

'I'm trying not to.' George kept her eyes fixed firmly on the queue of traffic in front of her. If she turned to face Whitney, her friend would be able to read the uncertainty in her eyes.

'Have you actually seen him since he asked?' Whitney pushed.

'We're due to go out at the weekend but I'm thinking about cancelling,' she admitted.

'Why?'

'Because I can't make up my mind what to say.' She hated feeling this way. She liked having order and control over everything in her life, and this was one of those situations which failed on both counts.

'But you must have at least thought about whether you're going to say yes,' Whitney continued.

'No. No. I don't know. I can't talk about it anymore, okay?' George flashed a helpless look in Whitney's direction.

'It's okay, I understand. Let's move on to today's visit. Our main concern is to find out about this incident Carly had to deal with on behalf of Julian Lyons. It could provide us with the motive.'

When they eventually arrived, they parked in the street and walked to the front entrance. They headed to the reception desk.

'We'd like to speak to Geraint Jones, please, Chelsea,' Whitney said.

The receptionist phoned him and, after waiting a few minutes, he came to meet them.

'I didn't expect to see you again so soon,' he said, smiling.

For someone who'd just lost his boss, he seemed remarkably upbeat. Had he taken over Carly's position already?

'Something has come to light which we'd like to speak to you about,' Whitney said.

'We can go to my office,' he said.

They followed in silence until reaching his office, and they sat around the circular table in the corner.

'We understand Carly dealt with an incident concerning Julian Lyons and one of the company's clients. What can you tell us about it?'

He frowned. 'I have no idea what you're talking about. I'm sure if Julian was involved in anything detrimental to the company I'd have been informed.'

'Brent Yates, Carly's partner, mentioned it. He knew very little, other than Julian Lyons had caused a big problem which needed her immediate attention.'

'Very strange. Did she inform Amelia?'

'I have no idea,' Whitney said.

'Can we look at his personnel file?' George asked.

He brought his laptop over to the table, opened it and called up a file. From her vantage point, George could see Julian Lyons' name, but couldn't make out any of the information.

'There's nothing in here about an incident,' Geraint said, after a few seconds staring at the screen. 'Brent must have been mistaken. Hang on, there's a sub-file on here. I'll look.' He frowned. 'It's password-protected. This is most unusual.'

'Can you get into it?' Whitney asked.

'I don't have the password. I'll have to ask Lizzie. She might know.' He returned to his desk and phoned her.

A few moments later she arrived.

'Lizzie, there's a password-protected file that we need to get into concerning Julian Lyons. Do you know anything about it?'

The girl coloured slightly. 'Yes, I do.'

'Why don't I?' he demanded, voice sharp.

Interesting. It didn't take much for his nastier side to appear.

Lizzie chewed on her bottom lip. George guessed this wasn't the first time he'd spoken to her in that manner. 'It was kept completely confidential. Carly dealt with it.'

'Tell me about it,' Geraint said.

Lizzie looked from Whitney back to Geraint. 'I'm not sure if I should say. Carly was most insistent about no one being told.'

'The man is dead. So is she,' Geraint snapped. 'I fail to see why rules of confidentiality should apply. It could be important in finding out who was responsible for the deaths.'

The girl still appeared uncertain.

'I agree,' Whitney said gently. 'We're dealing with two murders and this might be the reason behind it.'

'Okay.' Lizzie nodded. 'A complaint was made, against Julian Lyons, by one of our clients.'

'Is that it?' Geraint said. 'Clients moan all the time. He—'

'What was the complaint about?' Whitney asked, interrupting him.

'Julian allegedly sexually harassed a female employee of the company. Carly was very angry about his behaviour.'

'What happened? How was the situation resolved?' Whitney asked.

'I'm not sure exactly, but Carly did manage to get the complaint dropped.'

'And you've no idea what she did for that to happen?' Geraint asked.

'All I know is she went out of her way to make it go away, because we couldn't have a complaint like that against one of our partners. She said it would be too damaging to the company.'

George glanced at Whitney. What was the company involved in that this would have had such a catastrophic impact? As distasteful as it was, it wasn't unusual for charges of this nature to be made against staff members.

'Do you have the password to the file?' Geraint asked, pointing at his laptop screen.

'No, but I could have a guess at it. I did know many of Carly's passwords.'

'Okay.' He slid his laptop over to an empty space at the table.

She sat down and tried several combinations. 'That's strange,' she muttered. 'Oh, I know. Let me try this one.' She entered another password. 'I'm in,' she said, giving a satisfied smile.

Whitney pulled the laptop towards her. 'There's a signed document from the client, Weatherton, saying they're going to drop all allegations against Julian Lyons made by Erin Boyd. Nothing about the actual offence or any discussions between them. Why not?'

'I don't know. Maybe Carly didn't want to keep anything else on file, other than the signed document, in case they suddenly decided to take it further,' Lizzie said, averting her eyes.

She knew more than she was letting on. George was sure of it.

'So we still don't know how she persuaded them not to pursue it?' Whitney said.

'No.' Lizzie shook her head.

'This is all very unsatisfactory, and most irregular,' Geraint said.

'Agreed,' Whitney said. 'Thank you for your help, Lizzie.'

'You can go now,' Geraint said.

Lizzie hurried out of the office, appearing anxious to get away from Geraint.

Questioning her alone might produce more answers. She'd let Whitney know.

'Give me details of this client. We need to pay them a visit,' Whitney said to Geraint.

'Weatherton is a large haulage company. They've been a good client of ours for many years,' he said.

'Where are they based?' Whitney asked.

'Their head office is in Essex Street, the other side of the city.'

'What can you tell me about the work you do for them?'

'Very little. You'll need to speak to Rupert Lister, the senior partner in that division.'

'Please ask him to come down here,' Whitney said.

'I suspect you'll have to go to him. He doesn't deign to come here, unless he has to.'

Geraint certainly had a chip on his shoulder.

'Call him.'

They waited while he spoke to Rupert's PA.

'If you go up now he can see you, shortly. Would you like me to take you?'

'We know our way, thank you,' Whitney said.

They left his office and once out of earshot, George turned to Whitney.

'Do we have time to question Lizzie?'

'Why?'

'She was hiding something. She couldn't meet your eyes, and her words were rushed. Also, she couldn't get out of his office quick enough.'

'Okay. We passed her desk on the way to Geraint's office. We'll see if she's there.'

Lizzie was on the phone when they got there and Whitney signaled for her to end the call.

'Did you want me?' Lizzie asked once she'd finished.

'Can we go to the meeting room for a quick chat?' Whitney asked.

Lizzie glanced from side to side, as if checking no one was watching. 'Okay.'

'We believe you know more about the Julian Lyons situation than you were saying when you were in Geraint's office,' Whitney said, once they were seated.

'I've told you what I know,' Lizzie said, blushing.

'Dr Cavendish is an expert in body language. If she tells me you're hiding something, I believe her. What is it? We don't have time to waste,' Whitney said.

'I-I don't want to talk badly about a partner in the firm,' Lizzie said, quietly.

'Two people are dead. If you know something which could help find our killer, then you need to tell us,' Whitney said, a harsh tone to her voice.

George nudged Whitney with her foot. She was scaring the young woman. They wouldn't get anything out of her that way.

'Anything you do tell us will be confidential,' George said, hoping she wasn't overstepping her boundaries.

Whitney glanced at her. 'Yes, Dr Cavendish is right.'

Lizzie drew in a sharp breath. 'This wasn't the first time Julian had made unwelcome sexual advances.'

'There's nothing on his file,' Whitney said.

'That's because the woman in question was one of the lawyers here and she didn't make a formal complaint.'

'Who is this lawyer, we need to speak to her,' Whitney said.

'She no longer works here,' Lizzie said.

'We need her name,' Whitney said.

'But you said this was confidential,' Lizzie said, panic on her face.

'She won't know you gave us her name.'

'Miranda Moss. She now works at Brigstock.'

'How do you know about this?' George asked.

'Miranda and Carly were friends. They played netball together. I overheard them talking about it one day.'

'Do you know whether Miranda wanted to take it further?' Whitney asked.

'From what I heard, she told him where to get off and threatened that if he did it again, he'd be sorry. She didn't seem bothered, plus she was leaving.'

'Thank you for telling us,' Whitney said.

Lizzie left the room and George turned to Whitney. 'Added evidence of Lyons' nature. A sufficient motive?'

'We'll interview her and find out. Let's go and see Rupert Lister, he'll be waiting for us.'

When they arrived, his door was open, and he was seated at his desk. He glanced up and saw them.

'Come in, Chief Inspector.' He beckoned for them to enter.

'This is Dr Cavendish, she's a forensic psychologist and works with us on cases where we need her expertise,' Whitney said gesturing to George.

'How can I help you?' he asked.

'We've been talking with Geraint Jones about Julian. It seems there was a sexual harassment charge made against him by an employee of Weatherton. Are you aware of this?' He leant forward and stared at them; surprise reflected in his eyes.

'No. It's the first I've heard of it. What happened?'

'That's what we're going to find out. In his file is a signed declaration from Weatherton saying the accusation had been dropped and no further action would be taken. All we've been able to glean so far is it would be extremely damaging for the company if the matter were to be pursued. Can you enlighten us further?'

'No. I know nothing about it.'

'Can you think why it would be damaging to the company?'

'Any complaint can damage our reputation,' he said, dismissively.

'Did you work on any of their deals?' George asked.

'No.'

Why was he being so evasive? She hoped Whitney would pick up on it.

'You're a senior partner here. If we discover you've been withholding information which might help with our enquiries it will not bode well for you,' Whitney said.

'You can't threaten me,' he said, glaring at Whitney. 'If I say I don't know anything about this incident then you can take it as read.'

'No threats. Just a warning. We'll be back in touch after our visit to Weatherton, so you'd better not be lying to us.'

Chapter Seventeen

They left Hadleigh & Partners and set off for Essex Street where Weatherton was based. Excitement coursed through Whitney now they had a concrete lead to pursue.

'I think we're getting somewhere,' she said to George. 'I wouldn't be surprised if this sexual harassment charge has something to do with the murders.'

'We're certainly getting a picture of Julian Lyons. As we've already established, he's nothing like the man people have made him out to be. Adultery and harassment. What other secrets was he hiding? But why did Carly decide not to take these accusations further? Surely, it's not in Hadleigh's interest to employ someone like that.'

'I agree. Left to me, he would have been dismissed,' Whitney said.

'Also, what leverage did Carly have over Weatherton, or Erin, for them to agree to keep it quiet? It must have been something substantial,' George said.

'Yes. Erin was strong enough to make the accusation, but then agreed to have it all brushed under the carpet. I don't like the smell of it one little bit.'

Whitney hoped Erin hadn't been coerced into doing something she didn't want to. It certainly wouldn't be the first time that had happened.

'If Erin did it for the company, we'll find out once we speak to her,' George said. 'Do we know what position she holds there?'

'No. It wasn't on the file. All it had was her signature on the document and someone else's from Weatherton.'

'When do you want to interview Miranda Moss?' George asked.

'I'll sort that out after we've returned to the station.'

Once they arrived at Weatherton, they parked in the visitor car park which was to the side of the large 1960s four-storey office block. Behind the building was an enormous lorry park, which contained a selection of different sized trucks, from small to double length articulated lorries.

They pushed open the glass entrance door and headed up to reception.

'This is very different from Hadleigh's offices,' Whitney said.

'Yes. It's very utilitarian. No plush carpets and upmarket furniture,' George agreed.

'Detective Chief Inspector Walker and Dr Cavendish from Lenchester CID,' Whitney said when they reached the reception desk, holding out her warrant card. 'We'd like to speak to Erin Boyd.'

'I'll phone through to see if she's available,' the receptionist said.

It took several attempts before anyone answered.

'I've someone from the police here to see Erin.' She paused. 'Okay, thank you.' She ended the call and turned to Whitney. 'I'm sorry, she's in a meeting at the moment, and the departmental secretary said they can't be disturbed. Could you come back later? She should be free in an hour.'

Whitney tensed. What was it with some people that they thought they could dictate when she could interview someone? Did they think she had all the time in the world to wait for when it suited them? A visit from the police should take priority.

'No, we can't. Interrupt the meeting. We would like to speak to her urgently.' She emphasised the word *urgently* to make sure the message got through.

The receptionist blushed. 'I'll try again.' She phoned back. 'It's me. Interrupt the meeting and tell Erin she has to come down straightaway. It can't wait.' She paused. 'No. I don't know what it's about.' She ended the call. 'She'll be down shortly.'

They moved to the side by a noticeboard displaying information about the different staff activities the company had organised. It was bowling the coming weekend. Health and safety notices were also pinned up.

After almost ten minutes, and just before Whitney was about to go to the receptionist again, a woman who looked to be in her early thirties, came towards them. She was petite, pretty, with dark brown hair cut into a short pixie cut.

'Are you the police?' she said as she approached them. Concern showed in her eyes.

'Yes,' Whitney replied. 'I'm Detective Chief Inspector Walker and this is Dr Cavendish.'

'What's happened? Why are you here to see me?'

'We'd like to have a word with you in private. Is there somewhere we can go?'

'I'll check.' Erin went over to the reception desk. 'Is the interview room free?'

'Yes, it is. You can go in there,' the receptionist said.

'Okay, thanks.' She returned to where Whitney and George were waiting. 'This way.'

They followed as she hurried past offices with names on the doors. The interview room was small with a light oak circular table and six matching chairs. The white painted walls were bare, except for a large ordnance survey map of the United Kingdom.

'What is it? What's happened?' Erin blurted. 'Is this about Rich? Or my parents?'

'No, it's nothing to do with them,' Whitney said.

Erin's face visibly relaxed. 'Thank goodness. We've been through enough recently in the family. I couldn't face anything else.'

'What's happened?' Whitney asked, to check it wasn't related to the case.

'My father has recently been diagnosed with Parkinson's disease. It's been such a difficult time for him and my mum. They own a newsagents, but are putting it on the market because Dad can't work and Mum can't manage on her own.'

'I'm sorry to hear that,' Whitney said. 'We're actually here because we have some questions to ask you about Julian Lyons from Hadleigh & Partners. I take it you remember him?'

Her top lip curled. 'Of course I do. What's the bastard done now?'

'He's dead,' Whitney said.

'Dead?' she gasped.

'Yes. He died of a heart attack on Saturday.'

'Why are you telling me? No offence, but it's not like I'm interested.'

'This heart attack wasn't due to natural causes,' Whitney said, scrutinising her face for any signs of deceit.

'I still don't understand. Surely you don't think it's anything to do with me?' She shook her head.

'We understand from records we've viewed at Hadleigh & Partners that you made a complaint against him.' Whitney locked eyes with her.

'I did, yes.' She nodded.

'The person who dealt with the complaint, Carly Connor, is also dead.'

Her jaw dropped. 'Bloody hell. That's awful. But why do you think I could be involved? The complaint I made was ages ago. Last year.' She twiddled with the button on her cardigan.

'We're investigating all links between the two victims, and you're one of them. Can you tell us more about what happened between you and Julian Lyons, and how your complaint was dealt with?'

'I can, but I still don't see how it's related.'

Whitney gave an exasperated sigh. She was getting fed up with the girl continually denying it had anything to do with her. If she didn't answer her question soon, Whitney would start putting the pressure on. 'Just answer the question.'

Erin glanced at George and then back at Whitney. 'Hadleigh & Partners are our lawyers and last year they represented us in the takeover of another company.'

'How were you involved?' Whitney asked.

'I'm a paralegal in our in-house legal department.'

'If you have lawyers here why do you employ an outside firm?' Whitney asked.

'Our lawyers work alongside specialist lawyers in relation to certain deals.'

'What happened between you and Lyons?'

'There were some important documents which needed signing urgently and I went to Hadleigh's to collect them. It was early evening, and when I arrived the place was virtually empty. I went to Julian Lyons' office, as had been arranged, and he tried to force himself on me.'

Whitney's insides clenched. That sort of behaviour made her sick.

'I know it's not easy, but please could you tell us exactly what happened while you were there?'

She closed her eyes for a few seconds and drew in a breath. 'Before I realised what was happening, he'd closed the door. He then came over to me and began stroking my hair.

He was much bigger than me, but I managed to pull away and told him to stop.' Her fists were balled tightly, resting on the table. 'He backed off for a moment and I thought it would be okay. He then handed me the documents and as I took them, he grabbed hold of my wrist and pulled me towards him. He tried to kiss me, but I moved my head out of the way, while at the same time trying to pull out of his grasp. He told me he wouldn't take no for an answer and he knew we were attracted to each other.' Her voice cracked.

'I'm sorry to put you through this. But we have to know what happened next,' Whitney said.

'I twisted my arm and managed to get away from him. I shouted and threatened to knee him in the nuts if he took one step closer.'

'And then?'

'Thankfully, there was a noise from outside of the office, I'm not sure what it was, but it was enough to make him back off and sit on his chair.'

'What did you do?'

'I grabbed hold of the documents and left. I was shaking but wasn't going to let him see that. When I got back here I told my boss, who informed Hadleigh's HR department and they said they would handle it.'

'Did they?'

'A week later Carly Connor came to see me. She wanted me to drop the complaint.'

'Did she say why?' Whitney asked.

'She said that as nothing had *actually* happened, it would be in my best interest not to pursue it,' Erin replied.

'What did you say?'

'I was so stunned by her comments I could hardly string two words together.' Erin bowed her head.

'Did she say anything to qualify her position?' George asked.

'I got the impression it was important they didn't have anything tarnishing the company's reputation. But she didn't explain why.'

The hairs rose on Whitney's arms. 'Did they offer you anything to drop it? Money?'

'Nothing was offered, but she did say if I pursued the complaint it would be detrimental to my future career.'

'How?'

'She didn't elucidate, but I agreed not to take it further because I couldn't risk losing my job. I need the money.'

'Who was with you during the conversation with Carly Connor?' Whitney asked.

'No one. It was just the two of us. She said it was an informal chat and we didn't need to record it.'

'Did you tell your boss what had happened once she left?' Whitney asked.

'No. I just told him I'd decided not to take it any further.'

'Would it be fair to say you harboured ill feelings towards Julian Lyons and Carly Connor?' Whitney asked.

She knew it was stating the obvious, but she had to do

it. It wound her up that Carly Connor had used her position to intimidate someone. It was tantamount to bullying.

'Yes, but that doesn't mean I killed them,' Erin said.

'What were you doing on Saturday morning from around eight?'

Erin sighed. 'I was at home doing the housework in the morning and in the afternoon went for a walk'

'And Thursday morning from six?'

'At that time I would have been getting ready for work.'

'Can anyone vouch for you?' Whitney asked.

'My partner, Rich, can confirm where I was on Thursday morning, but not for Saturday as he was away on a football trip. They were playing a match down south. He left Friday evening.'

Whitney didn't believe Erin had anything to do with the murders, but still needed to cover all bases.

'We'll need to contact Rich. Please could you write down his mobile number?' She passed over her notebook and pen. 'If there's anything you think of that might help, please let me know,' Whitney said, handing over one of her cards, once Erin had returned the notebook.

'There won't be, but I want to reiterate that I was threatened to drop the complaint and did so because I didn't want to lose my job. That doesn't mean I murdered Carly and Julian, despite the company's bad practice.'

'Did you think about going for another job and leaving Weatherton?' Whitney asked.

'That's easier said than done. I have been looking for jobs, as it happens, but I'm not going to spoil my chances by whistle-blowing.'

'I understand. Thank you very much for your time.'

They left the meeting room together and once they'd reached the reception area, Erin headed back to her office and Whitney and George left the building for the car park.

'What an arsewipe Julian Lyons was. And Carly Connor wasn't much better. Keeping the harrassment quiet shouldn't be allowed. He should have lost his job because of it,' Whitney said, as they got into the car and drove away.

'Agreed. But we're certainly learning more about the victims and things aren't exactly as we thought they were,' George said. 'Both Julian and Carly acted unprofessionally.'

'We need to find out from Hadleigh's why it was so important to keep this incident quiet.'

Whitney turned her head and stared out of the window, tiredness washing over her. When interviewing, adrenaline kicked in and she got the job done. While sitting in the car relaxing, all the energy went out of her. She let out a sigh.

'How's your mum doing?' George asked.

She turned to George. 'She's fine. It's not her, it's me.'

'You're finding it difficult?'

'Yes, of course I am. To add cancer on top of everything else is the last straw. I've already told you this. Sorry, I didn't mean to snap,' she added, guilt coursing through her. George was only showing concern.

'When's your next appointment?'

'We're waiting for the results which they said would take up to a week. I'm hoping, if it's something really bad, we'll be contacted sooner.'

'Results probably won't come through quicker, whatever they are,' George said.

'Why not?'

'Because they need time to allow the cells to grow once they've tested them. There are some things you can't hurry.'

'How do you know this?'

'Remember I studied medicine before moving to forensic psychology?'

'Oh, yes, of course you did. I forgot. Until you discovered that you and blood didn't get on.' Whitney gave a half-smile.

'The less said about that, the better. I'm pretty good with blood now, though.'

'Would you ever think about going back into medicine?'

'Absolutely not,' George said. 'I love what I'm doing now, and I'm not going to change.'

'Anyway, back to the case. At the moment we seem to have a lot of mismatched parts to the investigation.'

'Up to a point. Julian Lyons is key. We know he had affairs and kept it quiet. We know he sexually assaulted someone and Carly Connor decided it was right to cover it up.'

'Once we find out the reason why, we should be closer to identifying our killer.'

'It crossed my mind that Hadleigh's might be in negotiations for a takeover,' George said. 'If so, they won't want any scandal attached to them.'

'Yes, but the incident was last year.'

'Takeovers can take months, sometimes years, to be finalised.'

'We'll get on to it once we're back.'

'You'll have to do it without me, I'm going back to work.'

'Okay. Are you available over the weekend? Oh no, you're seeing Ross,' she said remembering.

'I think I'll cancel.'

'You can't bury your head in the sand, George. You've got to face it and make a decision.'

'Easy for you to say. I can't make a decision without

thinking it through first. Which means looking at it from all sides. There's no point in me seeing Ross until it's straight in my head and I can give him an answer. He deserves that much.'

'If that's the way you want to play it, then that's what you should do. Drop me off at the station and we'll be in touch.'

Chapter Eighteen

Whitney walked into the incident room.

'Everybody, listen up. I want a run down on where we are. We have two bodies, both of whom worked at the same law firm and were involved in a cover up of Julian Lyons' activities. He sexually harassed a paralegal from another business, which was hushed up. Why? Ellie, see if you can identify a reason. George wondered if any takeover negotiations were going on.'

'Yes, guv,' Ellie said.

'Doug look into his victim's background. Her name is Erin Boyd. Check her social media. Finances. Friends. Anything you can find.'

'Yes, guv,' Doug said.

'We've also been informed of another lawyer Lyons harassed when she worked at Hadleigh's. Her name is Miranda Moss and she now works for a firm called Brigstock. Sue, find me the details, I want to pay her a visit.'

'Yes, guv,' Sue said.

'Is the motive linked to Julian Lyons' exploits? Are we to expect more deaths? We don't know.' She scanned the room, the frustrated expressions on the faces staring back echoing hers.

She walked over to the board where there was very little to show for their enquiries apart from two photos. Between them she wrote the names Erin Boyd and Miranda Moss, with arrows from each going to both victims.

'Guv,' Sue called out. 'I've got the address for Brigstock.'

'Thanks. Matt, stop what you're doing. You can come with me.'

'Okay, guv.'

They drove to Brigstock and headed inside.

When they reached the reception desk, Whitney held out her warrant card. 'We'd like to speak to Miranda Moss. Please call her for us.'

They waited while the receptionist spoke to Miranda. 'She can see you now for a few minutes. Her office is the second on the left.'

They walked in the direction the receptionist pointed and came to an open door. Whitney tapped gently and they walked in.

'Miranda Moss?' she said to the woman seated behind the desk.

'Yes.'

'I'm Detective Chief Inspector Walker and this is Detective Sergeant Price.' Whitney closed the door.

'How can I help you?' Miranda asked as she tucked strands of her light brown hair behind her ears.

'We'd like to talk to you about your time at Hadleigh & Partners.'

'Is this about Julian Lyons? I heard he'd died.'

'Yes, and also Carly Connor.'

'Carly?'

Whitney drew in a breath. 'I'm sorry to have to inform you, Carly died early yesterday morning.'

'Died?' Miranda whispered.

'We're treating her death as suspicious.'

'Why? What happened?'

'She had a heart attack while at the gym.'

'Why is that suspicious?'

'We're awaiting confirmation from the pathologist, but we believe she was given a substance which induced the attack.'

'I can't believe it. I only saw Carly last week at netball training. We'd planned to go for a drink after, but I cancelled because I had a headache.'

'When you last saw Carly, did she mention anything happening at work which she was worried about?'

'No. We had an agreement not to discuss work.'

'We understand that you had a run-in with Julian Lyons when he sexually harassed you.'

'How do you know?' Miranda pressed her lips together in a thin line.

'You were overheard discussing it with Carly.'

'I dealt with it. Why is it important?'

'It wasn't the first time Julian Lyons had sexually harassed someone.'

'Do you think it has something to do with his death?'

'We're not discounting it.'

'But how is that related to Carly?'

'What were you doing on Saturday morning from eight, and yesterday morning from six?' Whitney asked, not answering the question.

'On Saturday I was in Birmingham with my family. It was my sister's wedding. I went from work on Friday evening and returned home on Sunday afternoon. Yesterday, I was at home until eight and then came into work.'

'I'm assuming there's someone who can vouch for you?'

'My entire family. Am I a suspect?'

'We'd like to eliminate you from our enquiries. Please write down the name and number of someone we can contact.' She pulled out her notebook and slid it over to the woman.

'This is my parents' number,' Miranda said, passing back the notebook.

'The other incident of sexual harassment was hushed up by Carly. Can you think of any reason why?'

'No. It surprises me, knowing Carly. It can't have been easy for her. The reason must have been a strong one.'

'But you don't know what it is?'

'No, sorry.' Miranda glanced at her watch. 'I'm meeting a friend shortly for lunch, do you have any further questions?'

'Not for now. Thank you for your help.'

They left Brigstock and returned to Whitney's car.

'Well?' she asked Matt.

'I don't believe she had anything to do with the murders.'

'I agree. But, what we did find out is that Carly Connor was a principled person. Which makes it even more imperative that we discover what made her want to cover up the Erin Boyd incident.' She was distracted by Miranda walking out of the Brigstock office. 'Look. There she is.'

They watched as Miranda walked over to an older woman, with short grey hair, wearing a dark raincoat. Miranda put her arm around the woman, as if to comfort her.

'That must be the person she was meeting,' Matt said. 'She looks more like her mother than a friend.'

'Whoever it is, she seems upset about something.'

Miranda and the woman walked up the street, and into a nearby café.

'Do you want to follow them?' Matt asked.

'No. We don't want to be sidetracked. It's more important to get back to the station.'

Chapter Nineteen

'Doug, where are you in your investigation into Erin Boyd?' Whitney asked.

Four days had passed since Carly Connor's murder and their enquiries hadn't progressed. She'd been getting it in the ear from Jamieson and, in this instance, rightly so. It was ridiculous that after all their work they still hadn't got any further. They'd looked outside of the company to see if there was anything else connecting the victims, but there wasn't. Staff at Hadleigh's had remained tight-lipped over any disgruntled clients, insisting there were none for them to look into.

'I've examined her social media presence and there's nothing that stands out as being odd for someone of her age.'

'Like you would know what to look for in a woman of that age,' Frank quipped.

'You can talk,' Doug replied. 'I'm a lot younger than you are.'

'For goodness' sake, will the two of you give it a rest. It's like being in kindergarten. Just get on with your work.

We've two unsolved murders and that should take priority. Not your bickering.'

The pair of them stared at Whitney, open-mouthed. Had she been too harsh? She shouldn't take her frustrations out on them.

'Sorry, guv,' Frank said, hanging his head.

'Me too,' Doug said.

'I didn't mean to get on at you like that. I'm sorry, too. But we have to focus on finding the killer. Doug, what else did you come up with?'

'I looked into her finances and she certainly wasn't paid off. She pretty much lives from week to week and doesn't have any savings.'

'Which is more or less what she'd said to us.'

The phone rang on the desk by the board and Matt picked it up as he was passing. 'Price.' His body tensed. 'Thanks. We're onto it.' He replaced the phone. 'Guv, a body's been found at Hadleigh & Partners.'

Silence fell over the room and Whitney hitched in a breath.

Crap. Not another one.

'What do we know?' she asked.

'The victim is a senior associate in the corporate department and was found dead at his desk this morning.'

'You and I will go over there now. The rest of you continue with what you're doing. Do we have a name?'

'I wasn't given one. I'll phone downstairs and check,' he said.

She turned away, pulled out her phone and keyed in George's number. She answered after the first ring.

'We've got another death. Any chance you can meet us at Hadleigh's?' Whitney asked.

'This killer isn't wasting any time. Three deaths in a week. We might not yet know the exact motive but this certainly gives us food for thought. Is the killer sticking to a strict timeline through necessity?'

'Such as?'

'Only having a limited amount of time in the area. Or needing to kill within a time frame because it has meaning. Or getting off on the murders and being unable to hold back any longer. Although that's unlikely, simply because these murders appear to have been planned in advance. We certainly have some useful information to work with now.'

'I hope you're right. How many more people have got to die in that department before we can solve this?'

'Not a question I can answer,' George said.

'Can you meet me there?' she asked again.

'Yes. I've got a couple of things to do first and then I can leave. I should be there within the hour, traffic permitting.'

Whitney ended the call and headed over to Matt's desk. 'George is going to meet us there soon. Make sure scenes of crime officers and the pathologist are notified.'

'I've already done it, guv,' he said.

'Good. We'll leave now.'

'Do you still need me, if Dr Cavendish is going to be there?'

Whitney frowned. 'Am I missing something? Since when did you not want to come to a crime scene?'

'It's not that, do you remember I mentioned that Leigh has a follow-up appointment with the specialist later this morning? It would hardly be worth me going with you, as I'd only be there a short while.'

She could've kicked herself. Whitney had promised him anytime he needed to be with his wife he could go, no questions asked. It was the least she could do for him, as he'd been such a loyal sergeant over the years. Going over and above what most would do.

'I'm sorry, Matt. I was so preoccupied with the murder it totally went out of my head. Of course there's no point in you coming with me.'

'Thanks, guv,' Matt said.

She went over to Doug's desk. 'I want you to get together a team of officers and head to Hadleigh & Partners. I want a statement from everyone. No exceptions.'

'Do you know how many people work there?' he asked.

'Ellie,' she called out.

'Yes, guv?'

'How many people are employed at Hadleigh & Partners?'

'Three less than before,' Frank quipped.

'Frank. Enough. You're not helping,' Whitney snapped.

'Sorry, guv, it just slipped out.'

'One hundred and twenty,' Ellie said.

'Thanks.' She turned back to Doug. 'You'll need to take at least fifteen officers. I'm going now, and I'll see you there shortly.' She paused. 'Ellie, I want you to look into ex-employees of the firm. In particular those who used to work in the corporate department.'

'Yes, guv.'

'If this is down to one of them, it would certainly provide a reason for the HR director to be involved as well as members of the department.'

She returned to her office to pick up her coat and bag, and then left the station, driving herself to the law firm. When she arrived she was pleased to see proper procedures were in place and there was a cordon blocking off the entrance to the company car park. An officer was on duty outside the front of the building. She parked on the main road and headed to the entrance, where she signed the log and went inside. She strode up to the reception, where Chelsea was seated, her face pale.

'Is Amelia Harte here?' Whitney asked. 'I need to speak to her now.'

'I'll call her,' Chelsea said, her voice wobbly.

'My officers will be outside to make sure no one leaves the premises,' Whitney informed the young girl after she had finished on the phone.

'Okay.'

'Detective Chief Inspector.' Whitney turned as she heard her name being called and saw Amelia Harte hurrying towards her. 'Thank goodness you're here. This is dreadful. Lee Peters was found dead at his desk this morning. This can't continue.'

Lee Peters. So that's who it was. They'd interviewed him over Julian's death. Was there something more than work connecting them?

'My officers will be interviewing all members of staff. Do you have meeting areas where they can wait until statements have been taken?'

'Yes, one on each floor.'

'Please arrange for them all to be taken there and my officers will speak to them. I would like everyone to be accounted for.'

'Geraint can liaise with every departmental head.'

'I'll also need to be taken up to the crime scene. Has everybody vacated the offices close to the victim's?'

'I'll check,' Amelia said, turning and walking over to the reception desk. 'Contact Rupert Lister and ask him to come here immediately. Also, speak to Geraint in HR and instruct him to ensure everyone goes to the meeting room on their own particular floor.'

Chelsea carried out her instructions and shortly after Rupert Lister arrived. He nodded at Whitney.

'I want you to take Detective Chief Inspector Walker to the crime scene while I speak to the senior partners,' Amelia said.

'We'll be interviewing them, too,' Whitney said.

'I understand. We'll wait in the boardroom.'

'No one is allowed in or out of the building, apart from my officers. The offices will remain shut from now on.'

'When will we be able to reopen?' Amelia asked.

What was she saying, that business came first? Where was George when she needed her?

'I'll let you know. This is the third death, and that must take priority.'

Whitney turned to Chelsea. 'Our scenes of crime officers will be here shortly. Also the pathologist and Dr Cavendish. Send them straight up to the crime scene.'

'Okay,' Chelsea said.

She then turned to Amelia. 'Please keep in touch. Let me know when everybody is in their respective places.'

'What should the staff do once they've had their statements taken?' Amelia asked.

'Stay in the meeting rooms until they've been instructed they can go home.' Whitney turned to Rupert. 'Okay. Let's go.'

'Who found the body?' she asked as they entered the lift.

'Me.'

'Talk me through what happened,' Whitney said.

He drew in a breath. 'I went into Lee's office, as I wanted him to do some work for me, and found him slumped over his desk.'

'Does he have an office of his own?'

'He shares with one of our paralegals, but he's on leave this week.'

'And then what did you do?'

'At first, I thought he was asleep, so I called his name. When he didn't respond I walked around the desk. His face was turned, so it faced the window. His eyes were open and blank. I could see he was dead.' He leant against the lift walls.

'Did you touch the body?'

'Only his wrist. I called the emergency services and they told me to check for a pulse to see if he was still breathing. He wasn't. How could he be with his eyes staring the way they were? They told me to vacate the room.'

'Has anyone else been in the office?'

'Not that I know of.'

'Does the corporate department take up the whole of the fourth floor?'

'Yes.'

'Good. They'll be going to the meeting room to make their statements, but I also want to speak to them as a group,' she said.

They stepped out of the lift and Rupert took her to the victim.

'You can go back to your office,' she said to him, as she opened the door and stepped inside. Lee Peters was lying across the desk with his head resting on his arms. His blond hair flopped over his face. She pulled on her disposable gloves and walked over to him. His brown eyes were glazed over and lifeless. She shivered.

His jacket was hanging on the back of his chair and on the desk was a photo of a woman, holding a small baby, smiling at the camera. His wife?

There was a sound and she turned.

'Step away from the body,' Claire said as she pulled on her coveralls.

'I haven't touched anything,' Whitney said, jumping to

the side, as if she'd been caught doing something she shouldn't.

'Move out of the way and let me get on,' Claire said as she headed towards her.

Whitney made room for the pathologist to pass by. 'How are you, Claire?'

'I've been better,' the pathologist muttered.

'What's the matter?' She was surprised at the admission.

'It's not something I wish to talk about at the moment.'

'Okay, that's fine. But the offer's there if you want it.'

'I've got a decision to make and it's interfering with my work.' Claire gave a loud sigh.

'It's unusual for you to lose focus,' Whitney said.

'Agreed. I'll tell you. I've been offered another job.'

Whitney's heart sank. No. Claire couldn't leave. How would they manage without her?

'But you like it here?' she said, annoyed at her childish response.

'It would be nice to go somewhere I don't have to fight for any equipment I need. Where funding isn't restricted and I can get on and do my job instead of having to spend so much time doing unnecessary administration. It's very tempting.'

'We don't want you to leave,' Whitney said.

'I appreciate your support, but it's not your decision. I don't wish to discuss it further.'

'As I've already said, I'm here anytime you do want to talk,' Whitney said.

'I'll bear that in mind.' Claire went to the body and took its temperature. 'Estimated time of death between the hours of four and ten this morning. I'll give you a more precise time after he's back at the morgue.' She took out her camera and started taking snaps.

'Heart attack?' Whitney asked.

'I'm not going to justify that with a response. You know the drill.'

'May I come in?' Whitney turned and saw George standing outside the room.

'No, you can't,' Claire said. 'Wait until I've finished. There's hardly enough space in here for two, let alone three.'

'I'll leave you to it,' Whitney said as she went to speak to George. 'I'm pleased to see you here.'

'Has Claire confirmed the murder is the same as the others?'

'Well, obviously not, because she hasn't got the body back at the morgue. But it's got to be.'

'We'll know soon enough. Where are we going now?' George asked.

'Rupert Lister first. Then we'll address the department staff together. They must be frantic with worry. There's supposed to be a meeting of senior partners, but it might not have happened yet.'

They walked to Lister's office and found him sitting at his desk staring into space.

'Can we have a word?' Whitney asked as she knocked gently on the door and walked in.

'Come on in. Amelia has called a meeting in ten minutes' time, so I can't stay long.' He gestured for them to sit on the two chairs in front of his desk.

'We've had three deaths in a very short space of time. Can you think of any connection between the victims other than working for the same company, and Julian and Lee in the same department?'

'What do you mean?'

'Did they socialise away from work?'

'Not that I'm aware of.'

'Did Lee work closely with Julian on many deals?'

'They often worked together. Lee was a senior associate and he worked for both Julian and me. Does that mean I'm at risk?' His body tensed and panicked eyes stared back at her.

'We've no idea at the moment, but clearly everyone needs to be vigilant,' Whitney said.

'Were there any particular deals they worked on which were problematic?' George asked.

He visibly pulled himself together. 'We work on hundreds of deals a year. Some easier and more straight-forward than others. We have whole teams on each deal, so there would be more than just the two of them working together. No deal stands out as being more problematic than any other. There are usually issues with every one.'

Was he being deliberately evasive? Surely there was something he could tell them which would help.

'What about Carly Connor, how does she fit in with Julian and Lee?' Whitney asked, trying a different tack.

'I don't know of any connection, apart from the obvious.'

'Which is?'

'HR policies and procedures impact on all of us. Certainly, she wasn't part of a team working on a deal. I'm sorry I can't be of more use.' He looked at his watch. 'I can't stay for much longer.'

'We've confirmed that Carly covered up an incident between Julian and a woman from Weatherton,' Whitney said, ignoring his comment.

'Are you sure?' He frowned. 'Surely it would have been mentioned in the senior partners' meetings.'

'Yes, we're quite sure. We've spoken to the client and also seen Julian's personnel file.'

He shook his head. 'That's impossible. We have a

culture of transparency here. If he'd acted incorrectly, I'd have been told.'

'Not in this instance,' Whitney said.

He let out a frustrated sigh. 'What exactly did he do?'

'It's not something we're at liberty to discuss.'

'As a senior partner. I insist you tell me.' His tone was icy.

'You'll need to take it up with Amelia Harte.'

'I will. I should be aware of everything that happens in my department.' He glanced at his watch again.

Could Lee Peters also have done something Carly covered up?

'Can you check on the system and see if Lee's personal file is password-protected?' she asked.

'I'll take a look.' He pulled his laptop closer and opened it. 'No secret file. I have access to everything on him,' he said after a few seconds of looking. 'If there's nothing else, I must go.'

'We're going to speak to your whole department. I suggest you contact Amelia and explain you'll be down once we've finished, as I think you should be there. But before you do, we still have a few more questions. Is there something going on currently which involves the company needing to be seen as squeaky-clean?'

Would he tell them? She half-expected him to claim no knowledge on principle, seeing as he was angry about not being informed of the Julian Lyons incident.

'There have been talks of us merging,' Rupert said. 'We do need to be seen in the best light.'

Whitney exchanged a glance with George, who gave a knowing nod.

'What can you tell us about this merger?' Whitney asked.

'They're an international law firm who want to expand

into the area. It would be a good move for us, and sufficient reason for us to steer clear of any scandal. But if you say it involved Julian, then how did Lee fit in?'

'That's what we'll be investigating. How long had Lee worked here?'

'About three years. He was headhunted from a firm in Rugby.'

'Was he good at his job?' Whitney asked.

'Yes, exceptionally so. He was very well organised and conscientious. The best senior associate I've worked with.'

'Would it be unusual for him to be in the office early in the morning?'

'No, not at all.'

'Do you know what time he arrived today?'

'No. He might have pulled an all-nighter, although that's unlikely on a Sunday night. Or he could have come in early. I didn't arrive until eight. At nine I went to see him. His door was closed so no one would have known he was in there. As I've explained, I knocked, walked in, and found him dead.'

'Were many other people here when you arrived?'

'There were a few staff members. We officially operate a nine to nine-thirty start, but it's flexible based on the fact many of our staff stay late or come in early.'

She'd check the CCTV footage to see if that showed him arriving.

'Do you have his contact details to hand as we'll need to contact his family?'

'He's married to a delightful woman and they have a young baby. How the hell is she going to cope with a small child?' His voice drifted off and he stared into space.

'The details?' Whitney reminded him.

'Sorry.' He opened up his laptop and called out Lee's phone number and address, which Whitney wrote down.

'Contact Amelia and then go to the meeting room.'

'Okay,' he said. 'I'll be with you shortly.'

Whitney and George left him. 'As soon as we're done here, we'll go to the victim's family.'

'Why do you want to speak to the whole department together?' George asked.

'Just a hunch. Sometimes you can get more from a group than when people are on their own. They're going to be scared. Rightly so. Is our murderer picking them off one at a time?'

There were around thirty people seated at the table when they entered the room. It was eerily quiet. Whitney recognised Debbie, the secretary, who was situated to the left.

'Good morning. I'm Detective Chief Inspector Walker and this is Dr Cavendish. My officers will be here shortly to take statements, but I wanted to speak to you myself, first. It's been a very difficult time for all of you. Do you have any questions?'

'Yes. What's happening? Why are we being targeted?' an older man asked.

'That's what we're investigating.'

'Are we all at risk?' Debbie asked.

'Currently, we're unaware of the motive behind the deaths. We, therefore, suggest you make sure there is more than one person here at all times. Don't come in early, or stay late, if you're going to be alone.'

'On the news they said Julian and Carly were killed by lethal injection. Was Lee?' Debbie asked.

'We don't know at this stage. We have to wait for the pathologist to do the post-mortem,' Whitney said.

'When can we get back to work?' another staff member called out.

'Once our scenes of crime officers have completed

their forensic testing, and everyone has made a statement, we will be contacting the managing partner and a decision will be made regarding the reopening of the firm. It may take longer for this floor to reopen.'

'If that's the case, we will find alternative accommodation for everyone on another floor,' Rupert said.

Whitney glanced over her shoulder. She hadn't heard him enter the room. Next to him were a team of officers.

'If there are no more questions, we will begin taking statements.'

They left the meeting room, and Whitney instructed the team which offices they could use to take the individual statements. They then went downstairs to the main area just as Colin and Jenny from SOCO arrived.

'Hello,' Whitney said. 'Claire's with the victim at the moment. The office is small, so you'll need to wait until she's finished. But you can examine the rest of the floor housing the corporate department.'

'Will do,' Colin said.

She went to the reception desk. 'Chelsea, do you have CCTV on each floor?' she asked.

'No, I'm sorry, we don't. It's only outside by the front entrance and also by the back door.'

Why hadn't she checked that earlier?

'I want to see footage from the last two weeks. Send it to this email address.' She gave her a card.

'I'll need to speak to security first.'

'Do so. Tell them I want the footage this morning.'

'Okay.'

She turned to George. 'Now we'll head to the victim's family.'

Chapter Twenty

The victim lived in a small, modern, detached house on the outskirts of Lenchester. A new housing development which had caused a lot of unrest when it was built as it took away some of the beautiful countryside. But, politically, housing needs came first and despite the protests, planning permission had been given. Now there stood one hundred, identical, boxes.

'Is everything okay?' Whitney asked.

'Yes, I'm fine.' She tossed a quick glance in Whitney's direction before returning her gaze to the road.

'And you still haven't made your mind up yet about Ross, I assume.'

'Not yet. Let's concentrate on what's going on with the case.'

'Have you got anything you'd like to share, from a professional standpoint?'

'Initially, it pointed to the motive being to do with the business between Julian Lyons and Erin. But that could all change now we have the latest victim. Unless he was connected in some way to their situation.'

'Let's see what the wife has to say. If she'll be up to talking after we've delivered the news.' Whitney sighed. 'It never gets easier. The woman's life is going to be turned upside down. And they've got a small baby. How will she cope?'

'Maybe having the baby will make it easier.'

'Spoken as someone who doesn't have children. Don't bank on it.'

George parked in the driveway and they walked to the door and rang the bell. A young blonde haired woman, holding a baby, answered.

'Yes?' she said, looking at them both.

'Mrs Peters?' Whitney asked.

'Yes, I'm Ruby Peters.'

'I'm Detective Chief Inspector Whitney Walker and this is Dr Cavendish. We'd like to come in and speak to you.'

Panic crossed her face. 'Why, what's the matter? What's happened?'

'Can we come inside, please?' Whitney asked gently.

Ruby opened the door and they walked through the porch where there were pegs, with a selection of coats hanging, on one side and a mirror on the other.

'What is it?' she asked as they reached the hallway.

'We'd rather sit if we may?' Whitney said.

'Come through into the lounge.' She led them into a light and airy square room, which had a black L-shaped leather sofa and two matching chairs, all facing a large television.

'Can you tell me now?' Ruby lowered herself into a chair.

'I'm very sorry to inform you that there's been an incident at work. Your husband was found dead at his desk this morning.'

The words hung ominously in the air. George stared at the young mother to gauge her reaction.

'Dead?' Her arms tightened around the baby. 'How?'

'Let me take the baby,' George suggested.

The woman robotically held out her arms and George took the tiny sleeping child from her.

George had never held a baby before. Was she doing it right? She supported the head as she'd seen people do. The baby couldn't be more than a couple of months old. After settling, she carefully placed the tiny girl in the baby chair on the floor. There were straps, like a car seat belt, and she fastened them. Fortunately, the little one stayed asleep.

'At the moment, the pathologist is with Lee, but there have been two other deaths at the company recently,' Whitney said.

'Yes, I know. He told me about it. He was very upset about Julian. They'd often worked together.'

She was taking it very well, but George knew that it would hit her. There was no telling when that would be.

'The previous deaths were heart attacks, but they weren't brought on through natural causes. The pathologist will be looking to see if this was the case with Lee.'

'Oh, my God.' Her face paled and she began to shake. She wrapped her arms tightly around her body, but it didn't stop the convulsing.

'Is there someone we can get to be with you?' Whitney asked.

'M-my parents live around the corner,' she faltered.

'Would you like me to give them a call?' Whitney asked.

She nodded. 'Yes, please.' She picked up her phone which was on the sofa beside her and handed it to Whitney. 'They're on speed dial under Mum and Dad.' The baby stirred, which distracted her. She leant down and rocked the chair until the baby went back to sleep.

It was like she acted on autopilot.

Whitney left the room and returned very quickly. 'They'll be here shortly,' she said.

Ruby looked up and stared at Whitney, her eyes glassy. 'Thank you.'

'Are you up to answering a few more questions?' Whitney asked.

'Yes,' she said. She gently stroked the baby on the cheek and sat on the sofa close to her.

'What time did you last see Lee?' Whitney asked.

Ruby looked thoughtful for a few seconds. 'He had a call at around six this morning. He told me he had to go in to work straight away.'

'Did that happen often?'

'Occasionally he'd get a call first thing. It felt like he was at their beck and call. They expected him to drop everything and work when he was needed. Whatever else was going on in our lives.'

George's ears pricked up. What did she mean?

'Could you clarify?' George asked.

'They liked their pound of flesh. Employees earned every penny of their salary. They worked them hard. Too hard, I felt. Even when he was on paternity leave, he'd get daily phone calls.'

'Did Lee have the same view?' George asked.

'He didn't moan about it, if that's what you mean. He said other firms, especially in London, would work their lawyers much harder. It had got a little easier once he reached senior associate. The juniors worked longer hours. He wanted to make partner by the time he was thirty-five and this was the route. He accepted it more than I did.'

'Did he go into detail about the call?' Whitney asked.

'No.' She shook her head. 'I was busy changing the baby and didn't ask. I hardly even said goodbye.' Her voice broke.

'You didn't think it strange him having to go into work so suddenly?'

'No. If he was tied up with people from overseas on a different time zone then he would work outside of normal hours. It was nothing out of the ordinary.'

'And you definitely don't know why he had to go in to work?'

'No. I've already told you this.'

'Were you both in bed at the time of the phone call?'

'Lee was. I'd just got up because the baby was crying and needed changing and feeding.'

'What did Lee do after getting the call?'

'He showered, got dressed, and left.'

'And you definitely don't know who phoned? Did you overhear Lee using a name?'

'No. I was in the nursery so although I heard the phone ring, I couldn't hear him speaking.'

'Had there been any problems at work recently?' Whitney asked.

'Not that I know of. That doesn't mean there weren't any. My time's been taken up with Juno.' She nodded at the baby.

'How old is she?' Whitney asked.

'Ten weeks. And she's never going to know her daddy.' She emitted a low groan. 'What's going to happen now? I don't want to be on my own. I want Lee. I need him. *We* need him.' She buried her head in her hands and sat there rocking backwards and forwards.

The doorbell rang.

'I'll go,' George said, jumping up.

She opened the door to a man and woman, standing anxiously on the front step.

'Are you Ruby's parents?' George asked.

'Yes,' the man said.

'I'm Dr Cavendish. She's in the lounge with Detective Chief Inspector Walker.'

They rushed past George and hurried through the open door. Ruby's mother sat next to her daughter and pulled her into her arms, whispering soothing words. The dad stood behind the sofa, looking down on his wife and daughter, a dazed expression on his face.

'We'll leave you now,' Whitney said. 'I'm sorry for your loss.'

They left the house and went back to the car.

'Something obviously happened for him to be called into work early, and it wasn't anything that alerted him. We need to find out what it was. It also suggests he knew his assailant,' George said.

'His phone will help. I'm assuming he had it on him,' Whitney said. 'Let's go to the morgue and see Claire. She may have it.'

Chapter Twenty-One

When they arrived at the morgue Claire was standing with her hands on her hips in the main area, beside one of the stainless steel tables, staring at the body of Lee Peters. Whitney coughed, to attract her attention.

'What are you doing here?' The pathologist said, as she turned and frowned at them.

'Do you have the mobile phone belonging to the victim? He was called into work by someone, who we believe could either be the killer, or lead us to them,' Whitney said.

'I'm glad you're here. I have something to tell you. I was about to call,' Claire replied, not answering her question.

'What is it?'

'Death was from a heart attack and I found an injection site.'

Was that it? That wasn't anything they didn't already know.

'That's hardly a surprise,' Whitney said.

'Give me a chance.' Claire gave one of her trademark looks, designed to cut the recipient down to size. Although Whitney's skin had thickened as far as Claire was concerned, and she was no longer affected by it. 'I also believe there was a struggle. There was some trace evidence under the nails, which looked like make-up and skin cells. I'm having it tested.'

'More evidence that our murderer could be a woman,' Whitney said.

'Could be,' George agreed. 'But there are other reasons for why it was there. It could be from his wife.'

'True, except if you remember she wasn't wearing make-up when we saw her earlier,' Whitney said.

'In that case, he could have scratched the face of the killer when they came in to inject him,' George said.

'In your opinion, do you think he knew the murderer?' Whitney asked George.

'It certainly appears he did, considering he was prepared to drop everything and go into work early.'

'Which leads me to think it's someone who actually works at the law firm,' Whitney said.

'It could be, but what's niggling at the back of my mind is that the murders have been carried out at very peculiar times of day. Surely, if the person worked there, it would have been easier to murder at other times,' George said.

'Well, we should—'

'Excuse me,' Claire interrupted. 'This is my workplace. You can discuss your theories away from here. All you need to know from me is there's some interesting trace evidence which wasn't on the other victims.'

'Do you have the exact time of death now?' Whitney asked.

'I would say somewhere between seven and nine this morning.'

'And what about the phone, is it with his belongings?'

'Try over there.' Claire pointed to a stainless steel chest of drawers in the corner with a tray on top of it.

Whitney pulled on some disposable gloves and went over. She peered at the victim's belongings. 'Good, the phone's here. I'm going to take this with us, Claire.' She pressed the button and confirmed it was locked, before dropping it into an evidence bag.

'Right. Off you go, then. I'll email my report soon.'

'Nice seeing you, Claire,' Whitney said, to the pathologist's back as she'd turned away from them.

George and Whitney grinned at each other. Claire would never change. But the problem was, what if she took the other job? They left the morgue and walked down the corridor.

'I forgot to tell you, Claire mentioned to me earlier that she's thinking of taking another job,' Whitney said.

'Oh, that's very interesting.'

'Interesting? Is that all you can say? Catastrophic, more like. Still, I suppose it beats your other catchphrase: *fascinating.* Can you imagine how bad it would be for us if Claire goes? Remember the locum who messed up on the suicides that were really murders?'

'Yes, I do. But a locum is different from someone who's here all the time and is invested in doing a good job,' George said.

'You think locums aren't invested?'

'That's not what I'm saying.'

'Don't you think it's going to cause a problem? We know she's grumpy at times, but seriously, her work is a thousand times better than any other pathologist. Without her we're going to be totally up the creek without a paddle.'

'No, we won't be. If Claire leaves and you get someone

else, you'll learn to work with them. And you don't know she's definitely going to take the position yet, do you?'

'Stop being so rational. All I know is I'm going to send out vibes to make her decide to stay.'

'That's hardly going to work, is it?' George gave one of her patronising looks, which Whitney chose to ignore, mainly because her friend was correct.

'Right. We need to go back to the station so Ellie can run the phone through the self-service kiosk. Then we should find out who actually got in touch with him first thing.'

'Good idea.'

When they arrived at the station, they headed straight for Ellie's desk. She was talking to Doug. It didn't appear to be a work conversation as they were both laughing.

'Sorry to interrupt you two,' Whitney said. 'Ellie, I want you to take this phone belonging to Lee Peters, our third victim, and find out who called him at around six this morning and asked him to come into work. It was that phone call which led to him being murdered.'

'Yes, guv.' Ellie took the phone, and Whitney and George went over to the board.

'Listen up, everybody. Our latest information confirms our belief that the offender is a woman.'

'What have your learnt?' Doug asked.

'Claire's found some trace evidence under the nails of the victim. She believes it's make-up.'

'Or maybe the victim wore make-up himself,' Frank said.

'Yes, Frank, that's a possibility. Another possibility is he got it from his wife, but as she wasn't wearing any when we saw her, and we know he showered before leaving for work, it seems unlikely. At least now we've got something to work on, which is more than we had before. I've asked the law firm to email me their CCTV footage. They have one camera at the front of the building and one at the back.' She checked her phone. 'It's here. Frank, I'm going to send you the link. I want you to check to see what was going on outside of the law firm from six until nine this morning.'

'There's an awful lot to go through,' Frank said.

'You have somewhere else to be?' She arched an eyebrow.

'No, guv.'

'You'll manage. Do it quickly. There must be some-thing we can use from it. Doug, I want you to look further into Hadleigh & Partners itself. We've been told there's a possibility of them merging with another company, which I suspect is the reason Julian Lyons' exploits were kept quiet.'

'Do we have the name of the company they were nego-tiating with?' Doug asked.

'No, we don't. Supposedly the enquiry came through an agent. Contact Amelia Harte, managing partner at Hadleigh's, to find out the name of the agent involved. What about the interviews with all the staff? How are they going?'

'Our officers are still there,' Doug said.

'So why are you back here, then?' Whitney asked.

'I came back to sort something out,' Doug said, looking shifty.

She'd follow it up later.

'I need you back at the firm, keeping an eye on what's going on.'

'Yes, guv. I'll go now.'

'I've got the number which called the victim this morning a few minutes before six,' Ellie said.

'Great. Details?' Whitney said.

'None. It looks like it's a burner.'

'Can we tell where the call actually came from?' George asked.

'I'll look to see which towers it pinged,' Ellie said.

'Good. Have you got anything on ex-employees from the corporate department?' George asked.

'There's only one over the last two years. Casey Ryan who was on a temporary contract which was going to be renewed until it was discovered she'd been taking drugs while at work.'

Did she have a vendetta against the company? It would certainly be a motive.

'When did she leave?' Whitney asked.

'Mid-December, last year.'

'Do you know where she's working now?'

'She's on jobseeker's allowance, so she's not. Unless she's working on the side and not declaring it,' Ellie said.

'What else can you tell me about her?'

'She's twenty-nine and the address we have is her parents' house.'

'Send me her details.'

'Yes, guv.'

'I've got to see Jamieson. Can you hang around for a bit longer to visit this Casey Ryan?' she asked George.

'I'd rather you took someone else, so I can go back,' George said.

'No problem. When can you next come in?'

'I'm not one hundred per cent sure. It depends on what's going on at work. Call me.'

Whitney walked out of the incident room with George. 'How's it going with your ex in charge?'

'To be honest, it's not too bad at all. Better than I thought it would be. He seems to be leaving me alone.'

'Well, long may that continue,' Whitney said.

They parted ways when Whitney went upstairs to see Jamieson. His door was open when she arrived, and she walked in, giving a quick knock on the door.

'Do you have a moment, sir?' she asked.

'What is it, Walker?'

'I wasn't sure whether you'd been informed about a third murder at Hadleigh & Partners.'

'I've already explained how important that law firm is to us. Another murder is totally unacceptable,' he gave an exasperated sigh.

What did he expect her to do, wave a magic wand and prevent anyone else from being killed?

'I didn't ask for it to happen.'

'Don't be facetious, Walker. Where are you on the investigation?'

'The body was discovered this morning and currently we have several lines of enquiry underway.'

'Is Dr Cavendish helping?'

'When she can. She was with me today at the crime scene and when we went to see the latest victim's family.'

'Has she come up with a profile of our offender?'

'Not yet.'

'Well, ask her for one. Or what's the point in having support from a forensic psychologist?'

Whitney's jaw dropped. That was the first time she'd heard him say anything derogatory about George. In the past he'd worshipped the ground she walked on. Especially as, like him, she'd gone to Oxford University. Only she was more qualified, as she had a PhD. A fact that amused Whitney.

'She does more than simply profile. She aids us in our—'

The phone rang, interrupting her. 'I'm expecting this call, Walker. Next time we speak I want to hear there's been some progress. Close the door behind you.' He dismissed her with his usual flick of the hand.

She left his office, fuming. Where did he get off treating her like some inconsequential nobody? She might not be a superintendent, but she didn't get to chief inspector on a wing and a prayer. No. She'd worked her arse off for it and deserved his respect.

By the time she'd reached the incident room, she wasn't so angry. Helped by the coffee in her hand which she'd got from the vending machine on the way.

'Guv,' Ellie called out as she was passing, on the way to her office, to take a couple of minutes calming down time to rid herself of evil thoughts against Jamieson.

She changed direction and went over to the officer. 'You've got something?'

'Yes, I managed to track the tower where the phone call pinged. It's in the city centre, fairly close to the law firm,' Ellie said.

'Can you identify the exact location the call was made?'

'No. Not at this stage,' Ellie said.

'Okay. I was just wondering whether the offender was in a café watching, so they could see when our victim arrived. Are there any cafés open that early in the morning?'

'I expect so. I'll check to make sure. Alternatively, they could have been in their car waiting for the victim,' Ellie said.

'True. Although the murderer actually got into the building. So, why would they need to wait outside? It gets more bizarre by the second.'

'We'll get a break soon, guv. We always do.'

Whitney smiled and then headed over to Frank's desk,

changing her mind about sitting in her office. 'CCTV footage, Frank, where are we?'

'I've got something, guv.'

'Show me,' she said, perking up.

Frank pointed at his screen. 'Here's our victim arriving in his car. He drove up the side of the building and into the car park, which is around the back.'

'Yes, I see him.'

'Now, if we actually go back a few minutes before he arrived and look at the front of the building, there's a woman hanging around outside,' Frank said.

'Can we see her face?'

'No. She's looking down, as if she knows about the camera being there. But I'm sure she was definitely waiting for him. Five minutes after he drove his car towards the car park, she walked down by the side of the building.'

'She had to be going to the car park as there's nothing else down there, nor is there a way out.'

'Exactly. She must be our killer.'

'She could be someone who works there. Did you see any other cars drive into the car park?'

'No. He was the first, at seven-twenty, according to the footage.'

'Have you checked the camera in the car park itself? Can we see her go inside?'

'No, the camera doesn't pick her up.'

'Is that the same for our victim?'

'Yes, guv.'

Sue, who sat next to Frank, leant across and looked at the screen. 'Surely it has to be someone who works there if they have a key to the back door.'

'It's a swipe card system. Unfortunately, they are generic and not logged against individuals' names,

Whitney said. 'Can we see where the victim parked his car?'

'No, the camera is situated in a strange place.'

'Do you think someone deliberately moved the angle of it?' Sue asked.

'It's a possibility,' Whitney said. 'So, it appears that our murderer was able to convince Lee Peters to come into work early, and she waited for him to arrive and then followed him inside. Hmm.' She placed her hands on her hips as she stared at the image, thoughts charging through her head.

'We know it's someone with a swipe card to the building. Do they cancel cards belonging to employees who leave?' Sue asked.

'I don't know. Contact the firm and find out,' Whitney said. 'It could be an ex-employee if they don't. It wouldn't surprise me if cards aren't always cancelled, as some of these companies are really lax with their security.'

'Yes, guv. I'll do it now,' Sue said.

'Good work. We seem to be getting somewhere. All we need now is to identify this woman.'

Whitney walked over to the board and wrote *Murderer Woman?*

'Maybe it's someone who had an affair with Julian Lyons and wanted revenge,' Frank said.

'That's an option. But, if that's the case, why are victims two and three involved? It doesn't sit right. There's something else going on. Something we've missed. But we'll find it. I'll make sure we do.'

The door to the incident room opened and Matt walked in. He saw her and smiled when she beckoned him over.

'How did it go and what are you doing back here?' she

asked quietly, as the others weren't aware of the IVF treatment.

'Very well, thanks. We're hopeful for a positive outcome. I came back to see if you needed help.'

'Actually, I do. Ellie has given me details of a female ex-employee of Hadleigh's who worked in the corporate department. We'll go and interview her now.'

Chapter Twenty-Two

They took Matt's car to Casey Ryan's parents' house, a large detached property on the Pembroke Estate.

A woman in her sixties, with short blonde hair, answered the door when they knocked.

'I'm Detective Chief Inspector Walker and this is Detective Sergeant Price. We'd like to speak to Casey Ryan.'

The woman frowned. 'What's it regarding? I'm her mother.'

'We'd rather talk to Casey. We believe she may be able to help with our enquiries. Can you get her for us, please?'

'She's not here.'

'When are you expecting her home?'

The woman's face crumpled. 'I don't know. She doesn't tell us anything. We're having the most awful problems with her. Is she in trouble?'

It was like the woman had been bottling it all up and seeing the police there decided to let it all pour out. Did she know anything which might help the case?

'May we come in to talk?' Whitney asked.

Mrs Ryan opened the door and ushered them into a bright and airy hall. 'Come into the kitchen.'

They followed her into the large, square, modern kitchen which had a seating area in one corner, with a two-seater beige leather sofa and two matching easy chairs.

'Would you like a drink?' Mrs Ryan asked. 'Tea? Coffee?'

Whitney glanced at Matt. Did he have to rush off? She could murder a coffee. It seemed ages since her last one, even though it was probably no more than an hour. No wonder she was getting all twitchy.

'If you're having one, a coffee would be lovely. Thank you.'

'Not for me,' Matt said.

The woman put on the kettle and took out some mugs from the cupboard.

'Who lives here with you, Mrs Ryan?' Whitney asked.

'Please, call me Sylvia. My husband, Warren, and Casey. We have a son, but he lives in London.'

'Where's your husband at the moment?'

'He's at work. I'm not expecting him until after seven as he's got a late meeting. It was his first day back after our holiday.'

'What does he do?'

'He's a lawyer.'

'The same as Casey.'

A shadow crossed her face. 'Yes. But it didn't work out for her.'

The kettle boiled and Sylvia made the coffee. After giving Whitney hers, and keeping one for herself, she sat on one of the easy chairs, leaning forward slightly, both hands wrapped around her mug.

'We understand that Casey worked on a temporary basis for Hadleigh & Partners,' Whitney said.

'Yes, that's right. My husband knows Amelia Harte and as a favour they gave her a short-term contract in the corporate department.'

'Why was it only temporary?'

'Her work experience had been spotty, to say the least. She hadn't lasted long in jobs. When she first qualified, she worked in Birmingham, but that didn't last so she came back here.'

'Were the problems related to her drug use?' Whitney asked.

'Yes. She swore she'd come off them, and was very convincing, so we took her word for it. With hindsight, we were so desperate for her to turn her life around, we would've believed anything.' She closed her eyes for a moment and shook her head. 'How wrong we were.'

'How did they find out at Hadleigh's?' Whitney asked.

'They do regular drug testing and she was caught. It was near the end of her contract, which they were looking to renew, with a view to making her permanent, because she'd done a good job. But after failing the test they withdrew the offer. Why does she harm herself like this? Why?' Her voice broke. 'Sorry.'

Whitney picked up her coffee and took a sip, waiting for Sylvia to compose herself.

'What happened after she finished working there?' she asked.

'Nothing. Judging by her behaviour, I'm fairly certain she takes drugs most days,' Sylvia said, in a resigned voice.

'Do you know whether she's applied for any jobs?'

'Not to my knowledge. Warren refused to give her any money, to try to force her back into work, but instead she signed on for benefits. She's meant to go for interviews, but...' She shrugged.

'Do you know where she is at the moment?'

'I've no idea. She went out first thing this morning and said she didn't know when she'd be back. It's like this all the time. I don't know what to do about it. We persuaded her to go into rehab, and thought she was going to turn the corner. But she lasted all of one day and then left.'

'I'm really sorry for what you're having to go through. If we can't speak to Casey, maybe you will be able to help us. We're currently investigating several murders at Hadleigh & Partners.'

'Surely you can't think Casey has anything to do with it?'

'We're interviewing people who used to work there, which is why we'd like to speak to her. To eliminate her from our enquiries. Do you know where she was early in the mornings of Saturday the first, Thursday the sixth, and today?'

'I'm not sure of the exact time she went out this morning as I stayed in bed until ten and she'd already gone out when I came downstairs. As a rule, she doesn't usually get up early. We only came back from a holiday recently, so I don't know about Thursday.'

Not really a good alibi for this morning. She could have easily left early to carry out the murder.

'What about the first' Whitney prompted.

'I can't remember. Sorry.'

She took a sip of coffee and placed her mug on the table.

'Are you sure?' Whitney said gently. Was she trying not to drop her daughter in it?

She paused for a moment. 'Actually, I do remember. She went out late afternoon, but I'm not sure when she came home. We had to be at the airport by six on the Sunday morning so went to bed early. Yes. That's what

happened. So, she was here in the morning on the first'
Her shoulders relaxed.

'Where did you fly to?' Whitney asked.

'We have a villa in the south of France.'

Whitney stifled an envious sigh. She'd love a bolthole
overseas.

'You didn't mind leaving Casey on her own while you
were away, considering her drug taking?'

'We don't leave anything of value around. We're not
getting any younger and can't put our lives on hold just in
case Casey does something damaging. Having said that, we
don't go away for too long.'

'When you returned were there any problems?'
Whitney asked.

'No. The house was in good order.' Sylvia gave a wry
smile.

'When Casey goes out for the day, what time does she
usually come in?' Matt asked.

Whitney glanced at Matt. Was he trying to move the
conversation on because he wanted to get back to his wife?

'It's not regular. Sometimes she's back for dinner, and
others she's not back until we're in bed.'

'Who does she go out with?' Matt asked.

'We don't know. She never brings her friends home.'

'Mrs Ryan. Sylvia. We need to speak to Casey urgently.
When she comes home, please ask her to contact me
immediately. I'd like to see her at the station. Here's my
number.' Whitney handed her a card.

'My husband will want to be with her,' Sylvia said, as
she took it.

'That's perfectly fine. Do you have a recent photo of
Casey we could borrow?'

She wanted to compare Casey's build and demeanour

to the CCTV footage of the woman hanging around Hadleigh's.

'I have one on my phone.' Sylvia went over to the kitchen table and picked it up. 'I can email it to you.'

'Thank you. My address is on the card. If you do it now, we'll wait to ensure it gets through.'

Once the photo had arrived, they left and headed down the drive to the car.

'That was interesting,' Matt said.

'We'll circulate her details and hopefully she'll be brought in soon.'

Chapter Twenty-Three

'Contrary to how it's portrayed on screen, the work of a forensic psychologist doesn't just involve working up profiles of serial killers.'

George glanced around the lecture theatre at the students. Some were scribbling notes, while others had their phones on the table and were recording her. The rest appeared to be doing nothing other than sitting staring into space. This was the trouble with the introductory course, it attracted students who had no real interest in the subject, but had a gap in their timetable and needed the credit points. She imagined there would be a few dropouts once they were given their first assignment. That did tend to weed out the ones who'd planned to coast.

'The work, though interesting, is a lot wider and often mundane,' she continued. 'Forensic psychologists interact with a wide range of people. They—'

The door to the lecture theatre opened and Stephen marched in.

What did he want?

'Sorry to interrupt, Dr Cavendish.' He flashed one

of his infamous smiles in the direction of the students and then walked up to the lectern where she was standing.

'Yes?' she said in a clipped tone.

'Do you have time for a quick chat?'

She tensed. Time, yes. Inclination … a big fat no.

'You can see I'm in class,' she replied coolly.

'Come to my office after you finish.' He glanced at his watch. 'In fifteen minutes.'

'Fine,' she said.

He turned and left the room. It didn't take a brain of Britain to realise his actions were all done for effect. He wanted to show to her class that he was in a superior position. Well, bully for him. He must be feeling insecure if he had to resort to that.

Once her lecture was over, she picked up her bag, and headed to his office. His door was slightly open, so she walked in.

'Yes?'

'Sit down,' he said.

'What's the problem? I have work to do for my next lecture.'

'I'm sure you're totally prepared for it. As you always are.' An irritating grin appeared on his face.

'There's nothing wrong with being prepared for my work. Other people should follow my example, and maybe their students would do better.' She locked eyes with him, and he shifted awkwardly in his seat.

'I hope that's not a jibe at me.' He smiled.

To think she once found it disarming. Now she found it creepy.

'If the cap fits,' she said.

'Now, look here, George. I'm acting AP, so show a bit of respect or you'll suffer the consequences.'

It didn't take him long to show his true colours. He hated anyone making him feel inferior.

'What the hell is that meant to mean?' she said, her jaw tight.

She forced herself to relax. He wasn't going to rile her.

'Let's not get off on the wrong foot,' he said, a supercilious tone to his voice.

She drew in a breath. 'You called me in here. What is it you want?'

A smirk played around the corners of his mouth. 'I've discussed this with Robin.'

She groaned. The head of department getting involved wasn't good. He would do whatever Stephen asked, seeing as he hated confrontation and almost always rolled over.

'And?'

'*We're* not happy with the amount of time you spend working with the police on their cases.'

'Since when? I thought that was all settled? I've been using it for my research. My work hasn't suffered. My students are still doing well. What's the problem?' She glared at him.

'We believe it's not good for the university's reputation. We're an academic institution. We don't endorse staff members working alongside people in the *real world* to such an extent.' He made quote marks when he said *real world*.

She was so close to telling him where he could stick his quote marks.

'Why is this coming up now? Have there been any complaints?' she demanded to know.

'Not complaints, exactly.'

'What do you mean *exactly*? Have any students complained?'

'No, they haven't.'

'Of course they haven't, because all of my students do

well and they get a lot from me. More than from most lecturers. I mark their assignments quickly and I give them as much of my time as they need. If it's not the students. Who is it?'

'Well…' He paused.

'Has a member of staff complained?'

'Not exactly.'

'Here we go again with the *not exactly*. Who then?'

'There have been rumours.'

'Rumours? Explain,' she demanded.

'Look. I'm an associate professor, and you're only a senior lecturer. That means that if I have an issue, you do as I say. All you need to know is we're not happy with you spending so much time with the police.'

'We? Who is this *we*?'

'Departmental management.'

'That's bollocks.'

'Think what you like. We believe you should spend more time working here.'

'Doing what? What *extra* things am I not doing?' she challenged, knowing she was on very safe ground.

'You need to be seen.'

Could he come up with a more feeble response?

'Why?'

'Look, George, you don't have to like it, but you still have to do as I say, as I'm in charge.'

'No, you look, Stephen,' she said realising now what was behind it. 'This is all coming from you, isn't it? It's because I dumped you, and damaged your ego.'

'That's absolute nonsense,' he said. 'We split up over a year ago. Why would I become angry about it now?'

'Because you harbour a grudge. I know what you're like. To the outside world you're all smiles and friendly. But if you don't get your own way, then people know about it. I daresay you've been waiting all this time to find an excuse to do something to damage my reputation. I'll tell you now. Forget it. Because if you try to stop me working with the police or doing my job, I can assure you you'll have a fight on your hands. And I'll bring up everything you've done in the past. Be warned. The gloves are off.'

'Are you threatening me?'

'No need. I'm telling you exactly how it is.'

'Nice try, George. You can't do anything to me. Be sure to expect a written warning regarding your conduct, and you know what that means vis-à-vis your future.' He folded his arms, a self-satisfied smile on his face.

She stormed out of the room, slamming the door behind her, before she smacked the smug look off his face. She was so angry she could hardly contain herself. A state she rarely got into.

She marched to the head of department's office.

'Is he in?' she said to his assistant, Bea.

'Yes, he is but—'

She didn't give Bea time to finish as she strode past, gave a loud knock on his door, and opened it before waiting to be called.

'George. How can I help you?' Robin asked, closing his laptop and smiling.

'I've just been in with Stephen Grant, who's planning on giving me a written warning for not spending enough time at the university. Are you behind this?'

She stood there, with her hands on her hips, staring down at him. A deliberate move on her part to make him squirm.

'I didn't know about the written warning. That hadn't been discussed.' He couldn't maintain eye contact and glanced down to the side.

'I don't care whether you discussed it or not. The fact is

204

he told me I'm going to be given one. I will not tolerate it.'

'All we want is for you to pull back a bit on the time you're spending with the police.' His voice was weak.

'Why?'

'Because we feel that possibly your work here could suffer.'

'*Possibly*. What do you mean?'

'Umm…'

'I can assure you my work is not suffering. I'm working as hard as I've always done. I'm telling you now, Robin. I want this written warning rescinded or I'm going to human resources and will kick up a stink bigger than you've ever seen.'

'Don't be rash,' Robin said.

'Rash? Let me spell it out for you. I've single-handedly raised the department's research profile both nationally and internationally. My students have better results than most others. This is a vendetta against me by Stephen Grant because he couldn't stand being dumped. If this goes further, I'll make sure everyone knows, and I'm sure you won't want that.'

'Well…' Robin coughed.

'Just sort it out. Now.'

She marched out, leaving his door open, and went straight outside to get a breath of fresh air and to calm down.

What she wouldn't give for a cigarette. But she'd quit after going on a stop smoking course. How could she have been such an idiot as to have had a relationship with that bastard, Stephen?

One thing this whole episode had shown her was she didn't want to get involved with anyone ever again.

She'd say no to Ross's proposal. No way would she risk being put in such a compromising position again.

Chapter Twenty-Four

Whitney glanced up from her desk as Jamieson headed towards her office. What now? He opened the door and stared at her.

'Morning, sir. I was just about to come and see you.' She stood and walked around her desk until she was standing next to him. It made her feel more in control than when he loomed over her.

'You should have come sooner. I'm being pestered from all sides by people wanting to know exactly what's going on with these murders. Because they're my lawyers, they're expecting us to pull out all the stops. At the moment we're sitting on three deaths, and no nearer to solving them.'

'The third one has only just happened and we're investigating it. I fully appraised you of how the investigation was going on Monday.'

'You must have something else to tell me. I need to know before I meet with the Chief Superintendent later, as that's going to the be the first question I'm asked.'

'Since we spoke, we have examined CCTV footage belonging to the law firm around the time when the last victim went into work early Monday morning. There was a woman hanging around there.'

Had she mentioned the make-up and that they believed the killer could be female? What with everything else going on, she couldn't remember.

'Have you been able to identify this woman?'

'No. The cameras weren't in the right place.'

'Anything else? What has pathology come back with?'

'As you know, the killer injected the first two victims with potassium chloride in order to cause a heart attack. It's the same with the third victim. There was also some trace evidence found on the third victim. Make-up and skin traces under his fingernails, which is what confirmed our suspicions the murderer is most likely a woman.'

'But you're not one hundred per cent sure.'

'Not yet.'

'Why would somebody use a lethal injection as a means of murder? Have you looked into that?'

'It is something we're considering, and we will keep you up to date with anything new that comes up.'

'Have you found out how easy it is to access this drug?'

'Sir, we know what we're doing,' Whitney said through clenched teeth. 'We do need another press conference to let the media know we have a third victim. I came to see you yesterday about it, but you were out all day.'

'I told you I would be unavailable,' he said.

Crap. He had, and she'd forgotten all about it. It was his interview. How could she forget that?

'Yes, I remember now.'

She wasn't going to ask how it went. Despite wanting to know. He wasn't in the right frame of mind. He'll tell her soon enough once his promotion was official.

'It's only been two days since the murder. A press conference today will be fine,' he said.

'Yes, sir.'

'We'll tell the public we're seeking information about the woman hanging around. Email a screenshot of her to Melissa to send out to the reporters. Someone might recognise her even if we don't have a view of her face.'

'Will do.'

'I'll arrange for the media to come in later today, around two.'

Whitney swallowed hard. Today was the day she was going with her mother for the biopsy results. 'I'm tied up this afternoon. Unless we make it after four-thirty.'

'What are you doing?'

She didn't want to tell him, but it looked like she had no choice. 'I need to go with my mother for a hospital visit.'

'Can't someone else take her?'

'No, sir. We're going for the results of some tests she had and I want to be with her. She's not well and needs me there for reassurance.'

He'd better not say she couldn't go, or sparks would fly.

'What's wrong with her?'

Hadn't he had any supervisory training? Certain questions you don't ask of people you supervise. They should volunteer the information. But she'd have to tell him, now he'd asked. Or risk an almighty row.

'She may have cancer, which is why I want to go with her to hear the results.' The words stuck in her throat and she coughed to hide her discomfort. She didn't want him thinking she couldn't hold it together.

'Yes, of course, I understand, Walker. You must go.'

You could have knocked her down with a feather. Had the problems he'd been having with his daughter made him more compassionate?

'Thank you, sir.'

'But having said that, perhaps you should think about handing over the reins of this investigation to someone who can commit themselves to it full-time? What happens if it turns out that your mother has to have treatment? Are you going to want to be with her every time she goes?'

So much for him changing.

'I'll make that decision once we have the test results. Until then the situation is hypothetical.'

'I need to think about it now. If the tests turn out to be positive, then I'll decide whether to take you off the case immediately and appoint someone else.'

'I think you're pre-empting the situation,' she said, fighting back the tears. She wouldn't let him see her upset. It wasn't his words it was the way he was acting like it was a foregone conclusion. He thought her mum would have cancer.

Stop.

He was only being typical Jamieson. She dragged in a deep breath.

'I'll let you know when the press conference is confirmed,' he said.

He turned and walked out of her office, and she stared at his retreating back. She clenched her fists. How the hell could he turn around and do that to her? She thought they'd got over the threats of removing her from a case whenever something didn't go entirely as he wanted.

If her mother needed treatment, then of course she was going to be with her. But that didn't mean she couldn't do her job. She'd show him.

Whitney parked the car and took her mum into the breast clinic waiting room where they sat together in silence. She picked up a magazine from the low table in front of them, but the words and pictures kept merging into one. Her mind was going around and around in circles. What if her mum had cancer? What would they do?

'Don't worry, love,' her mum said, resting her hand on Whitney's arm. 'Everything will be okay.'

She turned and her mum was smiling at her. She pulled herself together. Acting like everything was over wasn't going to help.

'I know, Mum. Sorry, I was miles away, thinking about work.'

Blame it on work. A good excuse, and one her mum would believe. One thing she had realised, though, was Jamieson was right. She'd have to step back from work and take care of her mum. There was no one else to do it. She owed her that much for all the time she'd helped her and Tiffany.

'As long as it's not me you're worrying about.'

'Don't be daft, Mum. I know you're going to be fine.' She forced a smile.

'Mrs Walker?' Whitney looked up at the nurse who had come over to them.

'Yes,' Whitney said. 'I mean, I'm her daughter.'

'The doctor is ready for you now.'

'Come on, Mum.'

They followed the nurse to an office where behind the desk sat a woman who they hadn't seen before.

'Good afternoon,' she said. 'I'm Dr Randolph.' She smiled at them.

Whitney scrutinised her face. Was it a *good news* smile or an *I hate this part of the job* smile? She should be able to tell, the amount of bad news she'd given to people in the past. But today, she couldn't work it out.

'I'm Whitney Walker and this is my mum.'

'Please sit down.' She gestured to the two chairs in front of her desk.

The doctor looked at Whitney rather than her mum, which annoyed her. Just because her mum had dementia didn't mean she wasn't going to understand what was going on. Especially as today had been a good day.

'You're here regarding the results of the tests,' the doctor said, peering at the computer screen on her desk.

'Yes,' Whitney said, her body tense with anticipation.

'I have some good news for you. The lump we tested was benign.'

The tension in her body flooded out of her. If it hadn't been for the chair she was sitting on, she most likely would have collapsed in a heap on the floor.

'Thank goodness,' Whitney said, giving a loud sigh of relief.

'We will need to keep an eye on your mother in case any more lumps appear.'

'Of course, we understand.' Whitney turned to her mum, beaming. 'That's great news, isn't it?'

'Yes, dear. Very good news.'

Did she understand? It didn't matter. The main thing was her mum was going to be okay.

'Thank you very much,' she said turning to the doctor. 'It's such a relief.'

'You're welcome. Another appointment will be sent through in six months' time, and I would advise your mother keeps it.'

Whitney didn't need the advice. Her mum would be there for every appointment, no question.

'She will. Thanks again, you've made my day.'

'I'm glad,' the doctor said.

They left the room and it was like she was floating on air, her steps were so light.

'Thank goodness something's going right today,' she said grinning at her mum.

'What's happened?' her mum asked.

'Nothing I can't handle. A bit of trouble at work, that's all.' She didn't want to burden her mum and dampen things.

'Don't tell me, it's your boss.'

How did she know? It was incredibly observant of her mum considering how she'd been recently.

'Yes, but it doesn't matter because he's in the running for a promotion, which I'm hoping he gets. He's down to the last two, and as he was given the nod to apply, it's surely going to be his for the taking.'

'Fingers crossed he gets the job, then,' her mum said, holding up her hand and crossing her fingers.

Whitney glanced at her watch. She had hoped there'd be time to take her mum out for a celebratory coffee and cake, but there wasn't.

'I'll have to take you straight back home, because I've got a press conference to attend.'

'Another murder?'

''Fraid so.'

'I don't like you being around these murders all the time.'

'It's my job.'

'I know, but it must affect you.'

'I've learned to compartmentalise, and I've got a great team with me. We work the cases together, it doesn't all fall on my shoulders, so you don't have to worry.'

'Well I do. Thanks for bringing me here.'

'I'm your daughter. I'm not going to let you go with anyone else. Remember it's you and me against the world. That's what we've always said.'

'It's what you used to say to Tiffany.'

'It applies to you and me now as well,' Whitney said.

She dropped her mum at the home and headed into the city. She had thirty minutes before the press conference. She was in no mood to face Jamieson, as he'd get in the way of her enjoying the good news. She decided to stop for a quick coffee and meet him at the conference room rather than going to speak to him first. She was still angry about his comments from earlier. Okay, it was fine because her mum didn't need treatment and she wouldn't have to take time off. But that was beside the point. He should have been more supportive.

She made it back with one minute to spare and hurried down the corridor. He was standing next to Melissa, tapping his foot impatiently.

'Sorry I'm late, sir.' She didn't bother to give her usual *I got caught up on a call* excuse as he knew where she'd been.

'Well, you're here now. Come on, let's go in.'

No pleasantries, obviously. Or mention of her mum. Did she expect any other response? Actually, yes. But there was no time to entertain those thoughts now.

Melissa opened the door and they walked in. As usual, it was packed. Reporters at the front and camera crews at the back, with long, tall mics hanging over everyone's heads, able to pick up everything they said.

'Welcome, everyone,' Melissa said. 'Detective Superintendent Jamieson will take it from here.'

She passed over the mic and he pulled it in front of him.

'I have to inform you that we have a third murder victim from the law firm Hadleigh & Partners.'

'Is it an inside job?' a reporter in the front row called out.

'We're investigating all avenues,' Jamieson said.

Whitney turned to him. Yet again, he was answering a

question instead of passing over to her. Was someone watching his performance? It wouldn't surprise her if he was trying to make a good impression.

'Or someone with a vendetta against the firm,' the same reporter said.

'My previous answer covers that question. If any member of the public saw anyone in the vicinity of Hadleigh & Partners between the hours of six and nine on Monday morning, then please contact us. All calls will be confidential. In particular, we're looking for a woman who was seen close to the law firm, around six-thirty. Melissa will forward you a screenshot of this person of interest from the CCTV footage.'

'Can we have a name for the third victim?' a reporter called out.

'We're not releasing the name at the moment.'

'How was the person killed?' a voice came from the rear of the room.

Jamieson glanced at her. Did he want her to continue? If not, why have her there?

'The third victim was killed in the same way as the other two. A heart attack which was induced by a potassium chloride overdose,' he said.

'Would you say the murders were executions?' the same voice called out. 'And, if so, why?'

'We are still investigating and as yet don't have motives. If there are no more questions, then proceedings will be closed. Thank you all for coming in. We will keep you up to date with the investigation as and when we have anything further.'

As they left, Whitney turned to Jamieson. 'You didn't pass to me for questions.'

'No, I didn't, Walker, because I wasn't sure how things were going to be regarding you and the case. Whether you were going to be continuing in charge of the investigation, or it would be someone else. I thought I'd better take over in the interim.'

Really? That was the reason. Nothing to do with impressing the new bosses?

'That's ridiculous. In case you're interested, my mother's tests were clear, and everything will remain as it is.'

'I'm glad to hear it, Walker,' he said, walking away from her.

Was that the sum total of his concern? She hoped interpersonal skills weren't high on the list of desired attributes for the position he'd gone for or he'd have no chance at being promoted.

Chapter Twenty-Five

George stared out of the window, her hands in tight fists by her side, as she watched Ross park his car and walk up her short path to the front door. He waved and smiled when he saw her looking.

When she'd phoned and asked him to come over he'd agreed without asking why, even though he knew she didn't do anything without a purpose. She wasn't looking forward to the encounter as she had no desire to hurt him. But she had no choice. She was sure of that now. She'd debated suggesting they went out for a meal in a quiet country pub and she'd tell him there, but changed her mind as she didn't think delivering bad news in public was fair. She should have mentioned it to Whitney and asked for advice, but she suspected her friend would try to dissuade her from the course of action she'd decided upon.

Ross walked straight in, as he normally did, as she'd kept the door on the latch. He came into the lounge where she was still standing by the window.

'Hello.' She winced at the formality in her voice. Where did that come from?

'Hello.' He stood still, appearing uncertain what to do next, unlike when they usually met, and he'd come over and give her a kiss.

'I've made us supper,' she said.

'That's nice.' He held out the bottle of red wine in his hand. 'I've brought this.'

He followed her into the kitchen, and she finished preparing the fresh salmon with roasted vegetables. He poured two glasses of wine, handed one to her and sat down at the kitchen table.

'Come on, let's talk about this,' he said, gently. He picked up his glass and took a sip of wine.

'Don't you want to wait until after we've eaten?'

'No. You're all stiff and tense, so let's sort it now. I'm assuming your awkward manner is because you want to discuss my proposal. Sit down.' He gestured to the seat opposite him.

She sighed and did as he'd asked. He certainly knew her better than most other people. Was she doing the right thing?

'I think an awful lot of you, and I've enjoyed our relationship. We've been having a good time together. You know me very well, and you've let me do my own thing. But when you asked me to get married... I'm sorry, Ross ... I've thought of nothing else since you asked.'

'Yes, I thought you might. That's why you've been avoiding me.' The tight lines around his eyes tugged at her insides. She didn't want to hurt him.

'It's my way of dealing with things. I've come to a decision. My answer has to be no. I'm sorry.'

His face fell. 'What about if we move in together and skip the marriage bit?'

He didn't get it. It wasn't the piece of paper. If anything, that was the easy part.

'I had such a bad experience with Stephen, that it made me realise I'm happiest on my own.'

'Not all men are like Stephen.' He locked eyes with her. 'We're special together. Nothing about our relationship is anything like what you had with him.'

Could she feel any worse?

'But, I didn't know what *he* was like until he moved in.' Her heart ached, something she'd never experienced before. But she had to be rational about this.

'As I repeat, not all men are like Stephen. I understand. I can wait. I'll give you as much time as you need.'

'I don't need more time.'

'Okay, we'll carry on as we are.' The pained expression on his face belied his attempt to act as if it was all fine.

'No. We can't go back to how it was. It's not fair on you, because at the back of your mind you'll be thinking I'll change my mind.'

'Would it be so bad if you did?'

She wouldn't. Not now the decision had been made.

'I believe we should make a clean break.'

'So, you don't want to see me at all?' he said, an incredulous expression on his face.

'I'm going to miss you, but it's for the best.'

He stared at her, open-mouthed. His eyes full of anguish. She averted her gaze not able to witness his pain a moment longer.

She was doing the right thing, wasn't she?

'That's your opinion. I don't think it's for the best, but if that's what you want, and there's nothing I can do about it, then…then…' He stood and walked out of the room.

She thought he'd gone to the bathroom until she heard the click of the front door closing. She headed over to the window and watched him walk down the path and get into his car. She didn't move until he'd driven off and was out of sight.

She'd been so sure it was the best course of action. But now she was having doubts.

Her phone ringing distracted her. It was Whitney.

'Hello.'

'George?'

'Yes, of course. Who did you think it was?'

'It didn't sound like you. What's wrong?' Whitney sounded concerned.

'Nothing.'

'I don't believe you. What's happened?'

She'd have to tell her sometime. Now was as good a time as ever.

'Ross left after I told him I didn't want to get married.'

'He'll get over it. Probably his male ego getting in the way. Don't worry.'

Whitney hadn't understood what she'd meant.

'No, you don't get it. I've ended our relationship.' Why did saying it out loud make her feel so bad?

Whitney let out a small gasp. 'Why?'

'How could I carry on a relationship, knowing he wanted something I didn't? It's definitely for the best.'

'It doesn't sound like it from your voice.'

And this was why she much preferred to keep things to herself. So she didn't have to answer for all of her actions.

'What do you want, Whitney?'

'I phoned to tell you we have the results from my mum's tests.'

Crap. She'd forgotten all about that. 'I'm sorry for not asking. What were they?'

'The lump was benign and all they want to do is keep an eye on her from now on.' The relief in Whitney's voice was evident.

'I'm really pleased for you. That must be a weight off your mind.'

How could she have been so selfish as to wallow in self-pity over Ross, when Whitney had a real problem to deal with?

'It certainly was. It also means Jamieson will get off my back. Would you believe it, he actually turned around and told me he thought I should step down from the case because of Mum. I thought he'd got off that old hobby horse. But no, he was on it again. I told him categorically it wasn't going to happen.'

George smiled to herself. In some perverse way she'd miss the spats between Whitney and Jamieson. 'Hopefully he'll be gone soon. When does he hear?'

'Not soon enough, in my opinion.' Whitney laughed. 'He finds out next week, if not sooner. He said he's down to the last two. I can't think they'll keep him waiting too long. Also, you should have seen him in the press conference. All of a sudden he was taking over. He said it was because he didn't know what was going to happen with me. But I'm convinced it was because he knew it was going to be televised and he wanted his prospective new employers to see him in action.'

'That makes sense,' George said.

'Anyway, it doesn't matter. He's off my back for now. What's more important is you. Do you want me to come around? We can have a drink together.'

Did she? Actually, no. She'd rather be on her own.

'I don't think so. Thank you for asking, but all I want to do is settle down with a good book and try to put everything out of my mind.'

'You know, you are allowed to be upset even though it was your decision.'

'What do you mean?' She frowned.

'There will be a big gap in your life now there's no Ross. I'm still not sure why you decided to end it. Wasn't he prepared to stay as you were?'

'He was. I wasn't. How can we when he wants more than I'm prepared to give?'

'I don't get it. If he was willing to continue as you had been, then why would you turn him down.'

'Because he'd always be hoping I'd change my mind.'

'You don't know that. He loves you, and for him any time with you would be worth it. Don't you feel that way about him?'

'I can't deal with it.'

'Can't or won't? You're allowed to be confused, you know. It's what being human is all about.'

Not for her. She prided herself on not letting her emotions get in the way.

'We can discuss this another time.' It was all she could think of to stop Whitney from putting her on the spot.

'It's up to you. Are you sure you don't want me to come around?'

'No. I want to be on my own. It will give me time to process it.'

'Okay.'

'Thank you for calling and letting me know about your mother. I really appreciate it. I'm so pleased about the results.'

'When are we going to see you again? We've had a development with the case.'

'What?' George's ears pricked up, glad to have something else to think about.

'There's a lawyer who used to work in the corporate department, whose contract wasn't renewed because she was found to be on drugs.'

'That would give us our link to HR,' George said.

'Exactly. She looked the same build as the woman we're looking for from the CCTV footage. At the moment she's missing, but we're on the lookout for her. She has an alibi from her mother for the latest one, but it does seem a bit shaky. Hopefully we'll have her in custody by tomorrow. Her dad's a lawyer so everything has to be done by the book. I was hoping you could be there to observe when we interview her.'

'I don't know if I can get away tomorrow. There's something else I haven't told you. I had a big blow up at work with Stephen.'

'Bloody hell, it's all been happening for you. Was it that which made you decide to finish with Ross?'

Was she that transparent?

'It did contribute to my decision.'

'What did the bastard do?'

'He was lording over me in his *new* position and trying to get me to stop working with you. He got the head of department involved in his little scheme.'

'Crap.'

'Don't worry, I've got it sorted. When I go into work tomorrow, I'll make sure everything's okay. But if anything else happens, let me know and I'll be straight there. I'm not going to be dictated to by anyone, especially not Stephen Grant.'

Chapter Twenty-Six

I was concerned when I saw on the TV that they were looking for a woman who was hanging around outside the law firm when I went to see Lee Peters. But the image was so poor no one would recognise me.

Once I was in the building, I'd imagined someone might stop me and ask what I was doing, but there weren't many people around. Of course, having my own swipe card to get inside made it so much easier.

But even if the police are closing in on me, I'm not going to stop because I promised myself I'd get revenge. I will bring the rest of the deaths forward, though, just in case.

Am I overreacting?

Maybe. But I don't want to risk it.

They're not going to work out who I am from the CCTV. My head was down. And I made sure the camera angles were such that nothing around the back could be clearly seen.

I'll be more careful. That's all I can do. My victims will get their just desserts. They weren't chosen at random.

My life will never be the same again. I want their families to suffer like I did.

Someone's got to stop the way these law firms operate.

It's down to me to make it right.

What I'm doing will affect everyone in the legal profession.

Firms will realise they can't treat their employees the way they do and expect to get away with it.

Mark my words. I'll be thanked for having the courage to take a stand.

Chapter Twenty-Seven

Whitney parked outside the station. She was about to open the door when her phone rang. She picked it up from the passenger seat. It was Matt. Couldn't it wait, she was on her way to the incident room?

'Yes, Matt.'

'There's been another death.'

She tensed. Another death so soon? He had to be kidding.

'What do we know?' she said, emitting a sigh.

'Victim is male and was found in his car in the Hadleigh & Partners car park.'

'Okay. I'm heading there now.'

'Do you want me to come with you?' Matt asked.

'No. You contact Sylvia Ryan and see if Casey came home last night. I'll give George a call to see if she's available.'

George answered almost straight away.

'Hello.'

'Any chance you can get away?'

'Another death?' George asked.

'How did you know?' She ran her fingers through her hair.

'No pleasantries. Straightaway asking if I can come. You're always the same.'

'I'd no idea I'd become so predictable,' Whitney said.

'Where was the body found?'

'In Hadleigh's car park. I'm on my way. Hopefully Claire will be there soon, too. What about you?'

'I can be there in fifteen.'

'Thank goodness. Jamieson is going to go ballistic.'

It took her twenty-five minutes to reach the scene because of the heavy traffic. She'd spent the whole journey drumming her fingers impatiently on the steering wheel. Luckily, someone was on the ball as the car park had been cordoned off. A police officer was standing by the entrance.

Her phone rang, but she didn't recognise the number.

'Walker,' she said.

'It's Sylvia Ryan.'

Her heartbeat quickened. Was Casey at home?

'Hello, Sylvia.'

'I wanted to let you know that Casey went to visit a cousin in London yesterday and stayed the night. We're expecting her back later today.'

'Did you mention we want to interview her?'

'No. In case it stopped her from returning. I don't believe she had anything to do with the murders, but I didn't want to risk her not coming back.'

'Are you sure that's where she was?' Whitney asked.

'Yes. I phoned my sister, whose daughter Casey was with, and she said she'd seen them both. They're the same age and have always been close.'

'Thank you for letting me know.'

'I'll contact you when she arrives home.'

Whitney ended the call. If Casey was in London, she

was likely out of the frame for this latest murder. Were they ever going to get a break?

She got out of her car and headed over to the officer, who she recognised.

'Hello, Jade. Is everything in order?'

'Yes, guv. I've got the crime scene log and anyone attempting to enter the car park or building has been turned away.'

'Who else has arrived?' she asked, taking the log from the officer's hand and signing herself in.

'Dr Cavendish is in the car park and—'

'Don't worry, I can see who's here,' she said, having glanced at the names recorded and noting that George and Claire had both signed in. 'Have many people tried to come in?'

'Several, guv. But I directed them away without telling them what had happened.'

'Good.'

Whitney walked down the side of the building and into the car park. Claire was in her white coveralls talking to George. Whitney wandered over.

'What have we got?' she asked.

'And good morning to you, too.' Claire said.

'I know you don't like the pleasantries, so I skipped them,' Whitney said, giving a wry smile. 'Can I take a look?'

'Not yet. I've only just arrived. I was talking with George,' Claire replied.

Whitney looked across at George and arched an eyebrow. 'How come you get the preferential treatment?'

George shifted awkwardly from foot to foot. Had Claire been confiding in her?

'No reason. We arrived at the same time.'

'If you two can stand back for a while, I'm going to

take a look at the scene.' Claire leant over and pulled out her camera from its case. Whitney could see socks with elephants on them peeping out from the bottom of her trousers. A pair of giraffe earrings dangled from her ears, hitting the sides of her neck as she moved. Clearly the woman had an African theme going on. She stifled a giggle.

'We'll leave you to it. Call us when we're allowed back,' Whitney said.

She walked away with George until they were out of earshot.

'What was that all about with Claire? Is it anything to do with the job she's been offered?'

'Yes.'

'Is she going to take it?'

'She hasn't decided yet,' George said.

'It would be just my luck to lose her and keep Jamieson. We can't have that happening. What did you say to her?'

'Nothing. She wanted a sounding board, so I listened. I don't know whether she'll go or not. She's pretty fed up with the system at the moment.'

'We've got to do everything we can to keep her. She's the best pathologist we've ever had. Will *ever* have. Why don't you ask her out for a drink?' she suggested.

'Why would I want to do that?'

'Because you're similar in certain ways. Both clever. Tell her how much we would miss her. Do the *grass is always greener* stuff. She'll listen to you.'

'I'm not interfering. It's got to be Claire's decision.'

'Typical,' she said shaking her head.

'What do we know so far?' George said, in a tone that Whitney knew meant she'd finished discussing Claire.

'Nothing. I don't even have the victim's name or know who found him.'

'I believe it was someone who works there. She's standing by the entrance with one of your officers.'

Whitney glanced up and saw a uniformed officer with a young woman, who looked to be in her twenties. 'And you're only just telling me?' She threw her hands up in despair. 'I'll be back in a minute. I'm going to go over to see them.'

She walked to the entrance. 'I'm Detective Chief Inspector Walker,' she said to the woman.

'I'm Imogen Davis.' Her voice was barely above a whisper.

'I understand you're the person who found the deceased.'

'Yes.' The young woman's face crumpled, and tears rolled down her cheeks.

Whitney turned to the officer who she recognised as being relatively new in the job. 'We'll take Imogen inside and find somewhere to sit down and talk, rather than standing out here.'

The officer averted his gaze. 'Sorry, guv. I wasn't sure whether we were allowed in. I should have thought about that.'

'It doesn't matter. Let's go inside. Do you have a card to let us in?' she asked Imogen.

The girl nodded, pulled out a card and swiped. Whitney opened the door and ushered the woman in. The officer followed.

'Where can we go?' she asked Imogen.

'I'll find an empty office.'

Whitney debated calling George, then decided not to as she didn't want to leave Imogen.

'You can go now,' she said to the officer. 'Tell Dr

Cavendish where I am. Then stand by the back door in case anyone attempts to enter. Although they shouldn't as Jade is situated at the top of the drive.'

'Yes, guv.'

Once the officer had left, Whitney and Imogen went to the office.

'Please will you run through exactly what happened this morning,' Whitney said when they were both seated.

Imogen sniffed, pulled out a tissue and wiped her eyes.

'I arrived at half-past eight and drove down into the car park. I parked my car next to Tim's, as usual. I got out, looked over, and saw him slumped over the wheel of his car. I rushed around and opened the door. H-he stared at me, his eyes cold.' She shivered and wrapped her arms around herself.

'What did you do then?'

'I was glued to the spot, unable to take my eyes off of him. After a few seconds I managed to pull myself together and phoned the emergency services. They asked me if Tim was breathing and I told them no he didn't seem to be, and that his eyes were open and blank. I said he looked dead. They told me to close the car door to stop him from falling out.'

'Did you touch him?'

'No.'

'Then what did you do?' Whitney asked.

'I waited in my car until the police officers arrived and I told them what had happened.'

'Did you notice anyone hanging around when you were there?'

'No. We officially don't start until around nine-thirty although people do come earlier. When I arrived there was no one in the car park, only parked cars.'

'Are you a lawyer?'

'No. I work in the accounts department. Credit control.'

'And Tim?'

'He worked as a junior associate in the corporate department.'

What she'd expected.

'I need you to give a statement to one of my officers. Is there anyone who can wait with you?' Whitney asked.

'I'll text Shirley in my department and ask her to come down. I saw her car in the car park, so I know she's here.'

Whitney went outside to where George was standing.

'This is the third victim from the same department.'

'More bodies. More evidence,' George said.

'True. By the way, did you sort out your work issue?'

A smirk crossed George's face. 'You could say.'

'Tell me.'

'I went to see the head of department when I got in this morning and miraculously the written warning that was supposed to be issued was no more. Wise move on his part, because he wouldn't have relished the fall out.'

'I do believe you enjoyed it,' Whitney said, grinning.

'In a perverse way, yes I did.'

Whitney turned to see Claire putting her camera back in its case. 'Can we come over and take a look?' she called out.

'Yes.'

They headed over to the pathologist.

'What have you found so far?'

'Based on his temperature and rigor, I'd put time of death as somewhere between five and eight this morning.'

'So he could have been here for quite a while. What else can you tell me?'

'Nothing until we have the body back at the morgue. There's no obvious cause of death. I suspect a heart attack.

I'll look for an injection site and send the blood to toxicology.'

George frowned.

'What are you thinking?' Whitney asked.

'I keep going back to the mode of murder. Once we work out why it was used, then the pieces should slot into place.'

'Is it because it's not gruesome? Not all killers get off on seeing their victims suffer?'

'But if potassium chloride is administered without an anaesthetic, it's an excruciating way to die,' George said. 'It might not be gruesome, but the victims certainly suffered.

'Maybe it's because it's not difficult, like say strangling someone which needs strength. It's an easier option.'

'Not necessarily, because as we've already discussed the offender would have had to be in very close proximity to their victim in order to inject them.'

'So, they could've chosen an easier means, if they wanted to?' Whitney said.

'Exactly. Which means we have to identify what the injection symbolises.'

'Let's speak to Rupert Lister, if he's here. I fail to accept that no one can help us nail the motive for these murders. We're just not asking the right questions, or speaking to the right people. That's going to change now.'

Chapter Twenty-Eight

They went into the building. People were standing in huddles talking to each other in anxious tones. News of the latest death must have already circulated.

Whitney walked up to the reception desk where Chelsea sat staring into space. When she noticed Whitney she shook her head. 'I can't believe what's happened to Tim. When is it going to stop?'

'There are a lot of people in work today,' Whitney said, unable to answer the receptionist's question.

'They'd arrived before you stopped people from coming in. It was the same for me. I arrived at eight,' Chelsea said. 'Are they to be sent home?'

'Let them stay for now. What about in the corporate department? Do you know how many people are there?'

'I'm not sure. They moved back into their offices yesterday, apart from Lee's which still has the cordon up.'

'Please contact Rupert Lister and let him know we're here.'

They waited while she phoned.

'He asked for you to go up to see him. You know the

way. Here's a visitor swipe for the lift.'

They took the lift to the fourth floor and as they stepped out Lister was coming towards them.

'This can't go on,' he said, waving his arms in the air. 'The whole department will be decimated. You need to do something about it.'

Was that all he cared about? That the department would no longer be there. What about the victims and their families? She stared at him. How could he be so callous?

'Let's go to your office and talk. After that we'd like a word with Debbie.'

The secretary had steered them in the right direction before, with a little more probing she might be able to help them again.

'What can you tell me about Tim?' Whitney asked, once they were seated.

'He's twenty-seven and has been with us for three years.'

'Was he good at his job?' Whitney asked.

'Yes. He was the most sought after junior associate in the team.'

'His time of death has been put between five and eight this morning. Did he often come into work early?'

'I couldn't be specific regarding his arrival times but knowing his work ethic I would imagine he'd come in early, especially if he had deadline on a deal.'

'Can you find out what he was working on?'

Lister opened his laptop and after pressing the keys, peered at the screen. 'That's odd,' he said.

'What is?' Whitney asked.

'According to our work allocation records, currently he's not working on any big deals, so there was no need for him to be here early.'

'Could it be wrong?' Whitney asked.

'No. Every member of staff knows how important it is to keep the records up to date.'

'But he could come in early irrespective of what he was working on,' Whitney said.

'Yes.'

'We'll need to contact those close to him. Do you know his personal circumstances?'

'I believe he lives in a house with some friends.'

'Do you have the address?'

'I can get it for you.'

'We'll speak to them regarding the time he leaves for work. But first, we really need you to think about a common denominator between the three victims from your department. Maybe a deal they all worked on.'

'I'll have a look at the records. We have a lot of clients, and there are many deals going on at any one time. They could have quite easily been working with several clients together,' Lister said.

'We'll leave you for now as I want to speak to Debbie. Please text me Tim's address when you have it.' She handed him a card.

She didn't care that he was a senior partner, and the details could have been found by someone lower down in the organisation.

'Will do. We can't let this carry on. These deaths have to stop. Now it's in the press, we're losing clients. We've had a lot of phone calls asking what's happening and we can't afford to lose business.'

'Not only that,' Whitney said, glaring at him. 'It would be nice not to lose more members of staff.'

'Yes, of course I meant that, too. But equally, you know what I mean?'

No, she didn't. She kept that thought to herself,

though.

They left his office and went to see Debbie. She had known about Julian Lyons' affair, so she would likely know what else was going on.

'Hello, Debbie,' she said once they reached her. 'We'd like to have a word with you about Tim Collins.'

'I can't deal with this.' She swallowed hard. 'How can three people in the same department be dead?'

'That's what we're going to find out. I want you to think really carefully. Was there any deal they worked on together which was out of the ordinary? Anything you can recall that may help?'

'Many of our clients are demanding and these three could have worked on their deals.'

'Think hard. Does any deal in particular stand out?' Whitney pushed.

Debbie bit down on her bottom lip and was silent for a while. 'No. I'm sorry. Nothing springs to mind.'

'If you do remember anything, however inconsequential you think it is, then please contact me.'

'Definitely.'

Whitney's phone pinged and she glanced at the screen. 'It's the details for Tim Collins. We'll go to his house, now. I want to find out if his housemates know anything. We'll take your car,' she said to George.

They drove to the house, a 1930s terrace, in a predominantly student area of the city.

'Hopefully they haven't all gone to work,' Whitney said as they went up to the door and knocked.

Eventually a man who looked to be in his late twenties answered. His hair was dishevelled. Had they woken him up?

'I'm Detective Chief Inspector Walker and this is Dr Cavendish. We'd like to speak to you about Tim Collins.'

'What's he done now?' The guy laughed.

'Your name is?'

'I'm Dean Latimer. I was only joking about Tim,' he added, rubbing the back of his neck.

'We'd like to speak to you inside. Is there anyone else in?'

'No. It's just me. The others have gone to work. I worked late last night. I'm a chef and didn't get home until about two in the morning. Come in.'

He took them into the lounge which had dirty plates and cups on the floor, and clothes draped over the chairs. Whitney fought back the urge to wince.

'Sorry about the mess. We weren't expecting visitors.'

'That's fine. Please sit down,' Whitney said, gently.

'What's going on?'

She waited until they were all seated. 'I'm very sorry to tell you, but Tim has died.'

His body stiffened. 'How? Was it an accident?'

'We're treating his death as suspicious. The pathologist is with him now.'

'Is this anything to do with the other deaths at his workplace?'

'It might be. How much do you know about them?' Whitney asked.

'What I've seen on the news, and also Tim has spoken about it. He was very worried.'

Yet he went to work early on his own. Evidence that he knew his killer?

'Do you have details of his family?'

'No. All I know is his parents were divorced and he didn't see them. This is crazy. Tim dead.' He leant forward and rested his arms on his knees. 'What happened to him?'

'Another member of staff found him in his car at around eight-thirty this morning. But he could have been there for several hours. Do you know what time he left to go for work?'

'No, I don't.' He shook his head.

'Did he often go in early?'

'I couldn't tell you as I'm usually in bed when he leaves for work. It wouldn't surprise me if he did because it's such a busy place. He would often work late into the night. If you ask me, they took advantage of him because he was so good at his job.'

'It must have interfered with his social life.'

'He usually managed to juggle work with his music. He played in a band and his ambition was to get his music career off the ground. His job was well paid, and he used it to fund the band.'

'Did he have a partner?'

'He'd recently broken up with his girlfriend. They didn't go out for long. He wasn't the settling down kind.'

She could be worth interviewing.

'What else can you tell me about him?'

'He was a great guy. He had lots of friends, both men and women. He…' His voice faltered. 'I can't believe it.'

'Is there anyone we can contact to be with you?' Whitney asked.

'No. I'll be okay.'

'What about the others who live here, could they come home?' She hated the thought of him being alone, when he was so clearly in shock.

'There are two other guys. Fred and Will, I don't want to disturb them as they're both at work.'

'Can you let me have their details? We—'

She was interrupted by the sound of the front door opening. The lounge door opened and a guy walked in.

'I popped back home to collect my wallet. What's going on?'

'Fred, it's—' Dean's voice cracked.

'I'm Detective Chief Inspector Walker, please sit down. We have some bad news.'

Fred dropped down on the seat next to Dean and stared at her.

'What is it?'

'Tim was found dead this morning,' Whitney said.

'What?' His jaw dropped. 'How?'

'It appeared to be a heart attack. We're waiting for the pathologist to let us know. But we believe it might have been through a lethal injection and not natural causes.'

'Like the others in his department.'

'Yes, exactly.'

'I told him not to go to work until it was solved, but he thought he wouldn't get paid if he didn't go in.'

'Can you tell me what time Tim left for work?'

'Yes, I can. It was six-thirty. I'd got up to go to the loo and passed him heading down the stairs.'

'Was that his normal time for leaving?' Whitney asked.

'Pretty much, yes. He liked to go early because he could get a lot done.'

He had a pattern which made it much easier for the murderer.

'We'd like to take a look at Tim's room. Please could you take us?'

Dean took them upstairs, and Whitney handed George a pair of disposable gloves. Tim's room was small with only basic furniture: a bed, a chest of drawers, and a wardrobe. On the windowsill was a photo of several people at a ski resort. Whitney went over to have a look.

'Do you know who these people are?' she asked Dean.

He came over and stood beside her. 'That's Tim and his ex-girlfriend,' he said pointing to the two of them. 'I'm not sure who the others are.'

'Do you know when it was taken?'

'Fairly recently. He went over to France for a week's holiday last year. October, I think.'

She took the photo and put it in an evidence bag, then looked around the rest of the room. It wasn't very tidy, much the same as downstairs. In the wardrobe hung several shirts, a couple of jackets, and some trousers. In a pile on the bottom were jeans and T-shirts. Beside his bed was a book about Jimi Hendrix.

'He liked rock music?' she said.

'Yes, his band was rock.'

'Was he the singer?'

'No, he played bass guitar, but did everything and got it off the ground. He also wrote their songs.'

On top of the chest of drawers, she noticed some sheet music. They continued to look around, but there was nothing else of interest.

'Thank you very much for showing us,' she said. 'Please could you give me the name of his ex-girlfriend?'

'Lottie Harris, but how could she have had anything to do with it. She's already seeing someone else.'

'Is she still part of your social circle?' George asked.

'She's on the fringes.'

'Thank you very much for helping us. We're really sorry for your loss,' Whitney said.

They left the house and went to the car.

'Do you want to interview the ex-girlfriend?' George asked.

'Yes. But not yet. It's highly unlikely she had anything to do with it.' As they got in the car, her phone rang, interrupting them. 'Walker.'

'Is that the Chief Inspector?' a woman's voice said.

'Yes.'

'It's Debbie from Hadleigh & Partners. You said to call

if I remembered anything.'

Whitney put her phone on speaker, so George could hear, and rested it on the dashboard.

'Yes, Debbie.'

'I looked through all the deals over the last eighteen months to jog my memory and remembered there was one which drove everyone crazy because of the hours they all had to put in. We were dealing with three different law firms from all over the world, which meant there had to be someone here twenty-four-seven in case anything came in that needed attending to straightaway. The billable hours on that went through the roof. The client was livid.'

'Who was the client?' Whitney asked.

'I don't know if I can tell you. We sign a confidentiality agreement when we start working here.'

'Why don't you clear it with Rupert and then let me know,' Whitney said, not wanting her to clam up.

'Okay,' Debbie said, sounding relieved.

'In the meantime, can you remember who actually worked on the deal?' Whitney asked.

'Julian, Lee, and Tim did most of the work and—' She paused.

'Who did the rest?' Whitney prompted.

'There was Miranda Moss, another of our associates, who no longer works here. But that's not why I paused. I remember now there was also Victor Linfield. He was a newly qualified lawyer but wasn't with us for long because he passed away. It was very tragic for someone so young.'

The familiar tingle of excitement when she was getting somewhere, coursed through her veins. She called it gut instinct. George wouldn't agree, but she knew. It had happened too many times for it not to be real. They were onto something. She glanced at George who was staring intently at the phone.

'When did this happen?'

'About twelve months ago. I can't remember the exact date.'

'How did he die? Accident?'

'He had a heart defect which was affected by stress at work. His heart couldn't cope and gave up. I can't see how it can be anything to do with this though, as it happened so long ago.'

A heart attack? she mouthed to George, who shrugged.

'This is now the fourth death through heart attacks and only now Victor has been mentioned? Why?' Whitney asked, unable to hide her frustration.

'His heart gave up, I don't think it was a heart attack,' Debbie replied.

'What else could it be?' Whitney said.

'I don't know. I'm sorry.'

It was no good getting angry, that wouldn't help the investigation. At least now they had something else to work with.

'It might be nothing, but we still need to investigate it. Thank you.'

Whitney finished the call and pounded her fist on the dash.

'Can you believe these people? How could they have forgotten to mention this Victor?'

'Non-medical people might not have made the link,' George said.

'You're being too kind. Anyway, we need to get back to the incident room and get Ellie onto this.' Her phone pinged and she looked at the screen. 'This is from Debbie. The client whose deal they were working on was Lexicon, an international corporation. We need another chat with Miranda. We'll interview her after we've been back to the station.'

Chapter Twenty-Nine

They returned to the incident room and Whitney strode over to the board and wrote the names Tim Collins and Victor Linfield. Miranda's name was already there because of Julian Lyons' harassment of her.

'Attention, everyone. We're getting somewhere. There was a difficult case that they all worked on, not counting the HR director, who we'll park for the time being. It involved many hours work and the high number of hours billed caused a stink with the client. There were two others in the corporate department who worked on this case. Miranda Moss, who's now working at Brigstock and Victor Linfield who died unexpectedly about a year ago. According to the witness, Victor had a heart defect, discovered by the post-mortem. The defect meant his heart couldn't cope with the hours he was expected to work. We'll need confirmation of this.'

'Coincidence that they all worked on this difficult deal?' Frank asked.

Whitney glanced at George's face. The deadpan expression said it all.

'What do you think? Since when have we ever indulged ourselves in coincidences? We need to investigate. Ellie, find out what you can about this young man and what happened to him. Frank look into Lexicon, the client. In the meantime, I need to see Jamieson because he's going to be on our case again now we have a fourth victim. George, I'll leave you here with the others.'

She left them and went upstairs to Jamieson's office. She knocked on the door and walked in.

'Good morning, sir. I've come to let you know we've had a fourth murder.'

He might even surprise her by knowing. Though he rarely seemed to check the daily reports, at least not until later in the day.

'Another one, Walker? How many times do I have to tell you we need to get this sorted? How can one company have so many murders and you be no nearer solving them?'

'I wouldn't say that, sir.'

'What would you say? The murders are restricted to the firm, so someone must know what's going on.'

'Yes, sir. I understand that. But we're now getting somewhere. We've discovered all the victims worked on a particular deal that involved working crazy hours. We believe it's something to do with that.'

'What about the HR director?'

'We don't know yet how she fits in. I just wanted to let you know about the fourth victim and also where we are at the moment.'

'Next time make it more positive news.'

It was like he thought she sat on her arse all day long waiting for a clue to appear out of the ether.

'Yes, sir. Any news on the job?' She couldn't resist asking.

'I'm hoping to hear this afternoon. Thanks for asking.' He looked down at some papers on his desk. A signal for her to leave.

She returned downstairs, practically bouncing all the way. The day couldn't get much better. He was finally going to be leaving. She walked into the incident room and over to Ellie's desk.

'Found anything yet?'

'Yes. I've come across a newspaper article about young legal professionals dying of heart attacks. Victor Linfield is mentioned, as well as others from around the country. They talk about these deaths happening to young and fit individuals.'

'Except we know Victor had a heart defect.'

'That's not mentioned. But hardly surprising, as it doesn't make good copy. The journalist put it down to these people having to work long hours without a break over an extended period of time.'

Whitney called George over. She'd been standing at the board staring at it.

'Ellie's found an article about young law professionals dying from heart attacks when they were otherwise fit, and they believed it was the responsibility of the law firms because they were working them long hours without a break.'

'Sometimes eighteen hours a day for weeks on end, with no let up,' Ellie said.

'But that didn't happen in this firm, from what we can gather,' Whitney said.

'No, but when they were on the Lexicon deal, they worked long hours for weeks. If this is our motive, then the offender could certainly have blamed the firm,' George said.

'Exactly. It's all slotting into place,' Whitney said.

'Our murderer is sending us a message, which we hadn't realised until now.'

'And now you've sussed it?' Whitney asked.

'Yes. Potassium chloride is used because it induces a heart attack. Our killer is replicating what happened to Victor. The company was responsible for his death and now those who are deemed responsible are being subjected to the same fate.'

'Why was the HR director also singled out?' Whitney asked.

'The human resources department is responsible for the well-being of all staff. They allowed this to happen. Not only that, they were part of the employment process. Quite simply, the motive for these deaths is revenge.'

'Ellie, what have you found out about Victor Linfield?'

'He lived with his mother in Lenchester. Her name is Vera. She tried to bring a prosecution against Hadleigh & Partners for malpractice but it didn't even get to court. The fact Victor had a heart defect was to blame.'

'I still can't believe this is the first we've heard of it. Why didn't Rupert Lister think to tell us? Also, how come *we* didn't come across it.'

'I wasn't looking for it, guv. Sorry,' Ellie said.

'It's not your fault,' Whitney said. 'When did Victor die?'

'The twenty-eighth of February, last year.'

'Exactly a year before the death of Julian Lyons.'

'That was the trigger,' George said. 'There's usually something which sets it off, and this is it. The first anniversary of Victor's death. We've already established the killer is most likely a woman. I suggest the woman involved is his mother.'

'What have you got on Vera Linfield?' Whitney asked Ellie.

246

'She's fifty-five and works as a nurse at the hospital. Victor was her only child.'

'Is there a Mr Linfield?' Whitney asked.

'He died ten years ago,' Ellie said.

'And then she lost her son. It would be enough to send the sanest person over the edge.' Whitney shook her head. She could only imagine what the poor woman had gone through.

'I'm assuming working at the hospital means she'd have ready access to potassium chloride and syringes?' George said.

'So she wouldn't have needed to go online, which is why Ellie didn't find anything linking potassium chloride purchases with employees of the company,' Whitney said.

'Though if she had purchased online, we still wouldn't have established a link, because we had no knowledge of her or Victor at the time,' George said, correcting her.

'Do you have a photo of her,' Whitney asked.

'Yes, guv.' Ellie pulled one up on her screen.

Whitney stared at it. There was something familiar about the woman. It suddenly hit her. She looked like the woman they'd seen with Miranda Moss. 'Matt, over here,' she called to the detective sergeant.

'On my way, guv.'

'Do you recognise her?' She pointed to Ellie's screen.

'Yes, she was the friend Miranda Moss met outside of her office.'

'That's what I thought.'

'Are they in on the murders together?' Frank said.

'There was only one woman hanging around the law firm when Lee Peters was murdered,' George said.

'Yes. And the body build is more like Vera Linfield's than Miranda Moss,' Whitney said. 'But that doesn't mean Miranda isn't involved.'

'Or Vera is setting it up so she can murder Miranda,' George said.

'Yes, we have to consider that, too. Ellie text me Vera's home address. We'll try there first and if she isn't there, we'll see if she's at work. Are you able to come with me, George?'

'Yes. Count me in.'

Chapter Thirty

While driving, in her peripheral vision, George noticed Whitney staring ahead with a self-satisfied smile on her face. What was that all about?

'You seem in a very good mood,' she said.

'Well spotted. It's because later on today I'm going to find out that Jamieson is going to be on his way, and I can't stop thinking about it.'

'He got the position, then? You must be extremely pleased.'

'Not officially. He told me he was going to hear this afternoon. But we know it's going to be a yes. I can't wait for the official announcement. I'm going to celebrate big time tonight. You can come, too. It will be a double celebration because we'll have caught Vera Linfield. I can't see how life can get much better.'

'Okay. That's good.' George returned her concentration to the road ahead. If only things were so simple in her life.

'Oh, I'm sorry,' Whitney said. 'I forgot about you and Ross. How are you feeling about it now?'

How was she feeling? Strange. Out of sorts. She'd never experienced anything like it before. Understandably.

'To be perfectly honest, I'm feeling a bit down. But it was my decision and now I've got to live with it.' It sounded easy enough, so why was she struggling?

'Are you regretting it?'

'Not, per se. It was definitely for the best, even if it's not going to be easy.'

'You could always change your mind.'

'What will that achieve? Anyway, enough said on the matter.'

For once, Whitney took her words at face value and didn't try to interrogate her further. Thank goodness, because she wanted to block the whole thing from her mind.

They drove for a further fifteen minutes to an older part of the city, until arriving at a small, semi-detached, 1930s pebble-dashed house. The garden was neat and well-tended. If anything, it was too tidy. Straight away George could see that all the flowers and shrubs were regimentally planted at six inches apart. That told her a lot about the woman. Controlled. Methodical. Patient.

Whitney knocked on the door but there was no answer. They couldn't see through the front window as there were net curtains hanging, so they walked around the back, where the windows weren't covered. They peered into the dining room. Like the garden, everything was spotless and nothing out of place. A 1950s teak sideboard, with two cupboards and three central drawers, ran alongside the far wall. George stiffened. On the sideboard were some syringes standing up in a glass.

'Look at the back,' she said to Whitney. 'Can you see the syringes? Considering how tidy everywhere is, it's a weird place for her to keep them.'

'It gives us grounds to search the place.'

'Are you going to get a warrant, or break in?'

Whitney looked at her, a bemused expression on her face. 'We have no reason to break in. This will be done by the book. I'll get Jamieson onto the warrant and while we're waiting, we'll see if she's at work.'

They drove to Lenchester Hospital, walked in through the big double doors, and up to the reception desk.

'Can you tell me where nurse Vera Linfield works?'

'And you are?' The receptionist stared at her from over the top of her gold-rimmed glasses.

'Detective Chief Inspector Walker,' Whitney said.

'Hold on for a moment and I'll have a look.' After a few seconds she glanced up at them. 'She works on Warrington Ward in the haematology department.'

'Where's that?'

'Take the lift to the third floor and it's signposted.'

'Okay. Thanks.'

They found the ward and went to the desk.

'We're looking for Vera Linfield,' Whitney said to the nurse standing behind it.

'She's not at work today.'

'When's her next shift?'

'I'm not sure. Why are you asking?'

'I'm Detective Chief Inspector Walker and this is Dr Cavendish. We need to speak to her urgently.'

'I'll take a look at this week's rota.' She picked up a sheet of paper from a tray situated to her right and looked at it. 'She's due in tomorrow morning at seven.'

'Thank you,' Whitney said.

'Do you want to speak to any of the staff here?' George asked as they left.

'Not yet. I'm concerned about where Vera is. If she's not at work or at home could she be with Miranda Moss?'

'Except Miranda will be at work at this time of day,' George said.

'We'll go and speak to her. We need to find out more about her relationship with Vera. I'll ask Ellie to text me Miranda's address, in case she's not at the office.'

They drove to Brigstock and headed inside to the reception.

Whitney held out her warrant card as it wasn't the same receptionist they'd seen before. 'We'd like to speak to Miranda Moss. Please call her for us.'

The receptionist frowned. 'Her secondment at another firm started today. She'll be there for six months.'

'Do you know which one?' Whitney asked the receptionist.

'If you'd like to hold on a moment, I'll find out from HR.'

After a phone call, the receptionist turned to them. 'She's working in-house at Orton Asset Management Company.'

'I know where they're based,' Whitney said once they'd left. 'It's around the corner, we'll go there now.'

They walked quickly and within a couple of minutes had arrived at Orton.

'We're looking for Miranda Moss,' Whitney said, showing her warrant card to the man on reception. 'We believe that she started working here today.' He glanced at the card and back up at Whitney.

'You've just missed her,' he said.

'Where has she gone?' Whitney asked.

'She had an urgent phone call not long ago and had to rush home.'

'Did she say what was wrong? Whether it was a member of her family?'

'On her way out she mentioned a friend being in

trouble and said she hoped to be back in a couple of hours.'

Whitney's eyes narrowed. She was clearly thinking the same as George. Miranda could be in danger.

'Thank you for your help.'

'I don't believe Miranda is working with Vera,' George said, once they'd left. 'Vera has lured her from work on the pretence of there being an emergency. It's most unlikely that Miranda would leave work on the first day of a new job if they were planning on murdering someone else. All the other deaths have been planned.'

'Is there anyone else left to murder?' Whitney said.

'Miranda is the only one left on the actual team. The other person who might be at risk is Rupert Lister as he has overall responsibility for them.'

'Whether Miranda is a victim or in on the murders, find her and we'll find Vera,' Whitney said.

Once in the car, Whitney pulled out her phone and keyed in a number. She put the phone on speaker and rested it on the dash. 'Matt,' she said once he'd answered. 'I want you to bring Doug, Frank, and Sue and meet me at 25 Middle Street, which is where Miranda Moss lives. I want you there pronto, but no sirens.'

'Yes, guv.'

'We've got to go in there quietly. We don't know if Miranda is the next victim or working with Vera on the murders. Questions?'

'Where do you want us to park?' Matt said.

'We'll rendezvous away from the house. I'll get George to park twenty yards past it. At the moment we don't know for definite that Vera's there.'

'Yes, guv. Do you want me to inform the Super? He was looking for you not long ago.'

'Absolutely not. We'll see you soon.'

Chapter Thirty-One

George drove to Miranda's address and parked where Whitney had indicated. After a few minutes Matt, Doug, Sue, and Frank arrived in two cars and pulled up in front of them.

'You stay here,' Whitney said to George.

'Okay.'

She stared at George. She'd half-expected the psychologist to want to be a part of the operation, as she very often managed to get involved. But she didn't even ask. It had to be all the stuff with Ross. It had affected George more than she cared to admit.

Whitney got out of the car and walked over to her team.

'I think the best thing to do is have someone go to the front door and pretend to be visiting. I can't go because Miranda knows me, or if it's Vera, she might have seen me on TV at the press conferences. Sue, you do it. I want to see if we get an answer.'

'Okay, guv.'

Sue headed down the street, and up to the front door

of Miranda's terraced house. She knocked and waited, but there was no reply. She knocked again and then glanced over to Whitney who beckoned for her to come back.

'Could you see anything through the window?' she asked Sue, on her return.

'No, guv. But I didn't want to look.'

'We need to find a way in,' she said.

'There's an alleyway leading to the back of these houses,' Matt said.

'Okay. I'll go there with you, Matt, and the rest of you stay here. We'll keep in radio contact.'

Whitney and Matt walked down the side street, cut into the back alley, and found the gate belonging to Miranda's house. Luckily, it was unlocked, so they crept up through the rather overgrown garden and stood by the side of the back window.

The house was open-plan and she could see right through to the living area. Miranda was seated on the sofa with Vera sitting on an easy chair opposite. Vera was talking to Miranda and it seemed perfectly relaxed. So why didn't Miranda open the door when Sue knocked?

Whitney tried the backdoor. It was open.

'We're going in,' she said quietly into the radio. 'Frank and Sue, wait by the front door in case either of them decides to do a runner. Doug, stay on the pavement close by. There are no weapons visible, and they are sitting far enough apart that Vera can't inject Miranda when we enter, if that's her intention.'

Armed with her taser, Whitney opened the back door and slowly crept in, with Matt following. She accidentally knocked the bin and swallowed a curse as Miranda and Vera turned around.

'Police. Stay where you are and don't move,' Whitney said, stepping towards them.

'What's going on?' the younger woman said.

'Vera Linfield?' Whitney stared at the older, grey-haired woman.

She seemed relaxed and didn't appear to be planning to escape.

'Yes.'

'Both of you put your hands on your heads,' Whitney ordered.

The women obeyed. There was no syringe in sight. It was looking more like they had been in on this together.

'What's this about? You can't just barge into my house. It's not acceptable,' Miranda said.

'What are you doing here, Vera?' Whitney asked, ignoring her.

'I invited her. Why?' Miranda said.

'At work they said you'd come home because of an emergency.'

'Yes, that's right. Vera wanted my help.'

'That's a very understanding firm to allow you to leave because someone you know has a problem,' Whitney said. 'Especially on your first day there.'

'You don't understand. I'm all she has.'

'How do you know each other so well?'

'I knew her son Victor when I worked at Hadleigh's.'

'You worked on the Lexicon deal with him?'

'Yes. Why?'

'We suspect Vera is guilty of murdering all those involved in the deal Victor was working on before he died, and that you have been helping her.'

Miranda went deathly pale. 'Me?' She turned to Vera. 'Is this true?'

Vera remained silent.

'If you weren't involved then, we believe you were another person on her list,' Whitney said.

Miranda's eyes widened. 'No way. She wouldn't do that. Would you, Vera? Tell them you're not responsible for the murders.'

Whitney walked over to where the two women were sitting and took Vera's handbag. Inside, she found a syringe. She held it out for Vera to see.

'Does this contain potassium chloride?'

The woman nodded, her body slumped in the chair, the life having gone out of her.

'Vera Linfield, I'm arresting you on suspicion of the murders of Julian Lyons, Carly Connor, Lee Peters, and Tim Collins. You do not have to say anything, but it may harm your defence if you do not mention when questioned something which you later rely on in court. Anything you do say may be given in evidence. Do you understand?'

Vera nodded and didn't resist while being handcuffed. Whitney handed her over to Doug and Sue to take to the police station. She then called in George and they sat with Miranda, who was devoid of any colour. She kept muttering, 'I don't believe it,' to herself.

'How long have you been meeting with Vera?' Whitney asked.

'I connected with her after Victor had died. I felt really sorry for her. We struck up a friendship and she asked me to help prepare the case against Hadleigh's.'

'Even though you were working there?' Whitney asked.

'I did it in my free time. No one knew.' She bowed her head.

'Did you believe they were responsible?'

'Not really, but I couldn't leave her alone to fight them.'

'Did she tell you about her plans to kill everyone on the case?' George asked.

'No. I've been worried about her as she'd been

depressed recently because it was the anniversary of Victor's death. That's why I came home to meet her.'

'What was the emergency she called you about?' Whitney asked.

'She said she could no longer face living and was distraught. She said she needed to talk. I offered to go to her house, but she didn't want me to. She agreed to come here. Being new, my time was being taken up by various inductions into departments in the company, which is why I was allowed to leave.' She rubbed the heel of her palm against her chest. 'To think she murdered all the others. It's unbelievable.'

'And you had no idea that you were in danger?' Whitney asked.

A hollow laugh escaped her lips. 'I'd hardly agree to meet her if I knew that, would I? Why would she want to kill me, when I'm all she has?'

'The potassium chloride filled syringe is sufficient for us to believe your life was in danger. After the injection you would have had a heart attack like the others. Had she mentioned anything about trying to get her own back after what happened to Victor?'

'She sometimes talked about how Hadleigh's had caused Victor's death, but until recently it had seemed she'd started to accept it.'

'Did you tell her you thought the company was to blame?'

'I didn't say they weren't. But Victor had a heart defect which is why he died. He couldn't take as much stress as others of his age.'

'We'll need you to make a statement. Are you able to come down to the station?' Whitney asked.

'Yes.'

They all stood and as Miranda went to take a step, she

passed out. George caught her before she hit the ground and sat her down on the sofa, leaning her forward with her head between her legs.

'Take some deep breaths,' Whitney said.

'I'm sorry,' Miranda said, as she became more lucid. 'This has been such a shock. If you hadn't turned up, I might have been dead by now.'

'Well, we did. And now you're safe,' Whitney replied.

Chapter Thirty-Two

'Once Vera's lawyer arrives, you can go into the observation room while I interview her with Matt,' Whitney said to George, handing her a mic and earpiece as they stood in the incident room waiting for the call.

'As expected,' George said.

The phone on the desk rang and Matt answered it.

'Price.' He paused. 'Thank you. We'll be down shortly.' He replaced the handset. 'The lawyer's here now, guv.'

'Let's go.'

Whitney stared at Vera Linfield, her head bowed and her hands resting in her lap. What had her mental state been if she thought she could take the lives of all those other people as revenge for her son's death?

Whitney knew from experience that revenge took many different forms, so she wouldn't judge. She could have easily reacted in the same way if the psychotic twins who'd kidnapped Tiffany had murdered her. If that had happened, they wouldn't be alive today. She knew that with certainty. She forced those thoughts to the back of her mind, needing to concentrate on the interview.

'Interview on Friday, the thirteenth of March. Those present Detective Chief Inspector Walker, Detective Sergeant Price.' Whitney nodded at Vera and her solicitor. 'Please state your names for the recording.'

'Vera Linfield.'

'Francis Windham, solicitor.'

'Vera, I'd like to run through all the deaths. First of all, Julian Lyons.'

'He deserved to die,' Vera said, an icy tone to her voice.

'Can you please explain why?'

'He was the one who made sure my Victor died. He worked him seven days a week. Sometimes right through the night. Victor hardly slept. Lyons pushed him too far, while all of the time taking it easy himself.'

'Did Victor speak to Mr Lyons about his workload?'

'Of course he didn't,' she snapped. 'He was too scared. He wanted to succeed as a lawyer and Julian Lyons was a partner.'

'So you blamed Mr Lyons for the death of your son?'

'Him and other people.'

'What about Carly Connor, the HR director? Why did you target her?'

'Because I suggested to Victor that he should speak to her about the hours he was doing, to see if anything could be done to stop it.'

'Ask her if Victor agreed. I want to see if it was her idea or whether he wanted the long hours to stop,' George said in her ear.

'How did Victor feel about that?' Whitney asked.

'He didn't want to make a fuss, but I insisted. He always did as I asked.'

'What did Carly Connor say when he approached her?'

'She laughed and told him to deal with it as it's part of the job. The bitch.' Vera's top lip curled.

'There's no record of this interview anywhere,' Whitney said,

'The conversation was informal. I believe it took place in the canteen one lunchtime. How could she laugh? It's her fault, too, that he's dead. He would still be here if they'd done their job properly and not overworked their staff.'

'What about the others you killed?'

'They were just as bad because they kept piling work onto him because he was an NQ.'

'NQ?' Whitney asked.

'Newly qualified lawyer. The others working on the deal seemed to think they could dump all their work on Victor and he'd do it while they went home to rest.'

'And he explained all this to you, did he?'

'He did. He lived at home, so I saw what time he got back. I saw the state he was in. I begged him not to do it, but he said he'd be fine. But he wasn't fine. And one day that was it. They worked him so hard he died.' Tears filled her eyes, but she brushed them away with the back of her hand.

She hated her job sometimes. The woman was a murderer and deserved to be punished, but she'd been pushed beyond the point of no return.

'He did have a defect in his heart,' she said gently.

'They used that as an excuse. Yes, he had a heart defect, but that didn't mean what they did was right. They pushed him to his limit. They all deserved to die for what they did. They deserved to suffer. Their families deserve to suffer in exactly the same way as I have.'

'How did you manage to persuade Julian Lyons to go into the office on a Saturday?' Whitney asked.

'That was easy. I phoned and threatened to tell his wife about his *exploits*. Miranda had told me about what he'd done to her. He thought he was coming into the office to pay me off. As if I would take money from him.' Her nose wrinkled in contempt.

'What about the others?'

'I knew Carly Connor went to the gym every day. Miranda was friends with her, and she'd mentioned it. I followed her until I knew her routine. I slipped into the changing room without being seen and when Carly came out of the one next door, I called her in to help me. She didn't recognise me. It wasn't hard to inject her.'

'Lee?' Whitney asked.

'He thought I was coming in to talk about a memorial service for Victor. He was happy to meet with me early. I told him I had to get to work and it was the only time I could get there.'

'You chose a death that would have been extremely painful. Did you not have any compassion towards your innocent victims?' The words were out of Whitney's mouth before she could stop them.

'Innocent?' Vera snapped. 'There's only one innocent person in all of this and that's Victor. He's…he's…' She slumped down in the chair.

'Don't push it any further,' George said. 'She looks like she might break. She's admitted everything.'

Whitney gave an almost imperceptible nod. 'I can understand when you've got children, you want them to do well and you want the best for them. But what you've done hasn't brought Victor back. All you've done is made other families go through the pain and suffering that you did.'

The woman bent her head and wouldn't look Whitney in the eyes.

Whitney finished the interview and called for an officer to escort Vera back to her cell.

She went in to see George. 'It's sad. But you can't condone what she's done. Maybe now she can get some help.'

'Agreed,' George said.

'I've got paperwork to do. How about we meet up later for a drink and a chat?' she suggested.

'Good idea,' George said.

Whitney made her way back up to the office. This was turning out to be such a good day. She was practically dancing as she took the stairs two at a time. On her way she bumped into Jamieson.

'Hello, sir. We've interviewed Vera Linfield and she's admitted everything. Case closed.'

'Okay,' he replied, hardly looking at her.

She looked at him. What was wrong? He should be ecstatic.

'We'll arrange a press conference and announce that we have someone in custody. I thought you would have been pleased.'

'Well done, Walker,' he said.

'Is there something wrong?' she asked.

'Yes. I've just heard I didn't get the job.'

Her heart sank. He had to be kidding.

'I'm really sorry to hear that, sir. Especially as they'd given you the nod to apply. I thought it was yours for the taking.' What else could she say?

'You're not the only one. I don't wish to discuss it now. I'm going for a stiff drink. If anyone wants to know where I am, you don't know.'

'I never do, sir.'

'Don't be flippant Walker. I'm sure you're pleased to know I haven't been selected.'

'On the contrary, sir. I was hoping the job would be yours because I thought you were well suited to it.'

'Suited to it? What the hell do you know? I'm going. Make sure this doesn't get out because I'll know it's you if it does.'

Chapter Thirty-Three

George walked into the pub where she was due to be meeting Whitney. She scanned the room and saw the detective sitting in the corner with two drinks on the table. A pint of beer for her and a glass of wine for herself. She headed over, smiling.

'Hello. How are you?'

'Fine,' Whitney said.

George frowned. What was wrong?

'You don't sound fine. I expected to see you very happy and on top of the world.'

'I would be, except Jamieson didn't get the job.'

George sat down and took a sip of her beer. 'I thought you said it was a foregone conclusion. That he'd been given the nod to apply and the interviews were a formality.'

'It's what I believed, but maybe it was wishful thinking.'

'Yes, you formed a belief based on your imagination rather than rationality.'

'What? Don't start with all your fancy terminology.'

'I put into words your view of wishful thinking, that's

all. I know you're upset, but at least we've caught our murderer.'

'Yes, you're right. I've put up with Jamieson this long. I can carry on a bit longer. The trouble is, he's going to be like a bear with a sore head. And we all know what that means. He's going to be on my back all of the time for absolutely everything. He'll be a nightmare to deal with.'

'Come on, Whitney. You've dealt with worse than Jamieson. Pull yourself together.'

Whitney stared at her. 'Stop being so *George*, for once, and allow me an emotional breakdown.'

'I'd hardly call it a breakdown.'

'You know what I mean. It's been tough, especially with everything else that's been going on with Mum.'

'How is your mother?'

'She's doing well. I'm not sure she totally understood everything, but the main thing is she's going to be okay and not need any treatment, which is a huge relief. I really don't think I could have coped. It also means Tiffany doesn't have to come back until the twins' court case.'

'Yes, that is a plus. It's a long way for her to come back just to give evidence, though. And expensive.'

'Expenses will be paid by the prosecution. It's just the time factor.'

'Will she be allowed time off from work?'

'Yes. She's already agreed that with them. She'll come home for two weeks, which means we can spend some time together after the trial. You'll be able to see her, too.'

'I'd like that. Especially now I'm not seeing Ross.'

'How do you feel about it now?'

'I've put it to the back of my mind. I do miss him and will continue to for a while. But it had to be done. It's for the best.'

'I'm not sure I agree with you, but it's your decision.'

'Yes, it is. I do have some news which I think you'll be happy to hear.'

'What?'

'Claire texted me earlier. She's decided not to take the job.'

'Well, that's a relief,' Whitney said smiling.

'I thought you'd be pleased. Come on, let's drink up.' George clinked her glass on Whitney's. 'You've saved a life and caught a killer today. Here's to the next killer giving you some time off to relax.'

'Thanks, George.' Whitney rolled her eyes.

'What? Don't you want a rest?'

'Well, yes. But now you've jinxed it, which means there'll be another killer running around soon.'

∿

Book 7 - George and Whitney return in ***Ritual Demise***. The once tranquil woods in a picturesque part of Lenchester have become the bloody stage to a series of ritualistic murders. With the clock ticking they need to get inside the killer's head before it's too late.

∿

GET ANOTHER BOOK FOR FREE!

To instantly receive the free novella, ***The Night Shift***, featuring Whitney when she was a Detective Sergeant, ten years ago, sign up for Sally Rigby's free author newsletter at www.sallyrigby.com

Read more about Cavendish & Walker

DEADLY GAMES - Cavendish & Walker Book 1

A killer is playing cat and mouse....... and winning.

DCI Whitney Walker wants to save her career. Forensic psychologist, Dr Georgina Cavendish, wants to avenge the death of her student.

Sparks fly when real world policing meets academic theory, and it's not a pretty sight.

When two more bodies are discovered, Walker and Cavendish form an uneasy alliance. But are they in time to save the next victim?

Deadly Games is the first book in the Cavendish and Walker crime fiction series. If you like serial killer thrillers and psychological intrigue, then you'll love Sally Rigby's page-turning book.

Pick up *Deadly Games* today to read Cavendish & Walker's first case.

FATAL JUSTICE - Cavendish & Walker Book 2

A vigilante's on the loose, dishing out their kind of justice...

A string of mutilated bodies sees Detective Chief Inspector Whitney Walker back in action. But when she discovers the victims have all been grooming young girls, she fears a vigilante is on the loose. And while she understands the motive, no one is above the law.

Once again, she turns to forensic psychologist, Dr Georgina Cavendish, to unravel the cryptic clues. But will they be able to save the next victim from a gruesome death?

Fatal Justice is the second book in the Cavendish & Walker crime fiction series. If you like your mysteries dark, and with a twist, pick up a copy of Sally Rigby's book today.

∾

DEATH TRACK - Cavendish & Walker Book 3

Catch the train if you dare...

After a teenage boy is found dead on a Lenchester train, Detective Chief Inspector Whitney Walker believes they're being targeted by the notorious Carriage Killer, who chooses a local rail network, commits four murders, and moves on.

Against her wishes, Walker's boss brings in officers from another force to help the investigation and prevent more deaths, but she's forced to defend her team against this outside interference.

Forensic psychologist, Dr Georgina Cavendish, is by her side in an attempt to bring to an end this killing spree. But how can they get into the mind of a killer who has already killed twelve times in two years without leaving a single clue behind?

For fans of Rachel Abbott, L J Ross and Angela Marsons, *Death Track* is the third in the Cavendish & Walker series. A gripping serial killer thriller that will have you hooked.

~

LETHAL SECRET - Cavendish & Walker Book 4

Someone has a secret. A secret worth killing for....

When a series of suicides, linked to the Wellness Spirit Centre, turn out to be murder, it brings together DCI Whitney Walker and forensic psychologist Dr Georgina Cavendish for another investigation. But as they delve deeper, they come across a tangle of secrets and the very real risk that the killer will strike again.

As the clock ticks down, the only way forward is to infiltrate the centre. But the outcome is disastrous, in more ways than one.

For fans of Angela Marsons, Rachel Abbott and M A Comley, *Lethal Secret* is the fourth book in the Cavendish & Walker crime fiction series.

~

LAST BREATH - Cavendish & Walker Book 5

Has the Lenchester Strangler returned?

When a murderer leaves a familiar pink scarf as his calling card, Detective Chief Inspector Whitney Walker is forced to dig into a cold case, not sure if she's looking for a killer or a copycat.

With a growing pile of bodies, and no clues, she turns to forensic psychologist, Dr Georgina Cavendish, despite their relationship being at an all-time low.

Can they overcome the bad blood between them to solve the

unsolvable?

For fans of Rachel Abbott, Angela Marsons and M A Comley, *Last Breath* is the fifth book in the Cavendish & Walker crime fiction series.

∼

RITUAL DEMISE - Cavendish & Walker Book 7

Someone is watching…. No one is safe

The once tranquil woods in a picturesque part of Lenchester have become the bloody stage to a series of ritualistic murders. With no suspects, Detective Chief Inspector Whitney Walker is once again forced to call on the services of forensic psychologist Dr Georgina Cavendish.

But this murderer isn't like any they've faced before. The murders are highly elaborate, but different in their own way and, with the clock ticking, they need to get inside the killer's head before it's too late.

For fans of Angela Marsons, Rachel Abbott and L J Ross. Ritual Demise is the seventh book in the Cavendish & Walker crime fiction series.

Acknowledgments

As usual, I'd like to thank my friends and critique partners, Amanda Ashby and Christina Phillips, for being there at all times of day and night when I need help.

Emma Mitchell, thank you for being the best editor ever. This series wouldn't exist without your amazing input.

Thanks also to Kate Noble and my Advanced Reader Team for your fantastic help in getting the book ready for publication.

What can I say about the cover, except Stuart Bache, once again, has nailed it. Thanks so much.

And, of course, no book would be complete without mentioning my fabulous family Garry, Alicia, and Marcus. Thanks for all your support.

About the Author

Sally Rigby was born in Northampton, in the UK. She has always had the travel bug, and after living in both Manchester and London, eventually moved overseas. From 2001 she has lived with her family in New Zealand, which she considers to be the most beautiful place in the world. During this time she also lived for five years in Australia.

Sally has always loved crime fiction books, films and TV programmes, and has a particular fascination with the psychology of serial killers.

Sally loves to hear from her readers, so do feel free to get in touch via her website www.sallyrigby.com

Made in the USA
Middletown, DE
19 July 2022

69676942R00168